Butterfly Kisses

Linda L Brown

Published by Linda L Brown, 2014.

Butterfly Kisses
By: Linda L Brown

Published by Linda L Brown at Smashwords
Edited by Felicia Brown-Eaton
Copyright 2014 Linda L Brown
Cover Design by Mistress of Manipulation at Selfpubbookcovers
Smashwords Edition, License Notes

The First Snow

The dishwasher hummed its own musical tune as Cassandra leaned against the counter drying her hands. With a quiet sigh she thought about all the other things left to do before Christmas morning. There were presents to wrap, stockings to fill, and cookies to decorate. As her eyes fixated on the cooling cookies a pair of brown shoes entered the kitchen. They crept closer towards Cassandra as if on a mission. Then just inches away they stopped.

Cassandra seemed oblivious to the intruder. At least until she heard a creek in proximity. She nearly jumped out of her skin, but when her eyes fell upon her husband, she snapped him with the towel. "Damn you, Sean! You practically scared the living daylights out of me."

"Whoa, wait a minute;" Sean cried out when he saw his wife reading the towel for another strike, "It's not my fault you didn't see me come in."

It was true. He had been in plain sight. So why did she not see or hear him? While she pondered on the question her husband went back to the cupboard. But it didn't take long for her to realize her mind was elsewhere. She placed the towel on the counter then with sincerity she apologized. His warm gentle smile told her he had accepted. And when he went back to collect the last two mugs, she became aware of the night's ritual.

With her husband taking care of the hot cocoa, she decided to take a break. As she walked towards the dining room she felt a slight prick on her buttock. In a flash she spun around. And when she saw the devious grin on her husband's face, she couldn't believe he had just pinched her. Realizing his playful intensions, she shook her finger at him then turned and walked away.

She entered the dining room as the sound of running water reached her ears. It seemed everything was running smoothly. That was until she noticed the tablecloth was slightly draped more over to one side. For her everything had a place, and everything had to be in place. So unable to control the urge she walked over and fixed it. With that now out of the way she headed for her resting place.

As she made her way into the living room, she was surprised to find her eight-year-old son and six-year-old daughter quietly putting a puzzle together on the floor. Their polite behavior made her wonder if they were behaving because they were told to. Or was it due to Santa's impending visit? Either way she was pleased to have the quietness. With the desire to keep it that way she carefully walked past them.

When she finally reached the sofa, she plopped down. Then after taking a moment to breathe, she leaned towards the coffee table and picked up the book she had placed there earlier. Ready to pick up where she left off, she scooted back and raised her knees close to her. She then rested the book against her legs and was about to open to the marked page when something caught the corner of her eye.

Through the small opening between the curtains, she saw the bright icy white outline of a face staring back at her. Frightened she almost screamed, but then she realized what it really was. Sure, delight bubbled within her as she turned towards her children and said, "It looks like snow this year kids."

Upon hearing the word SNOW, Ronnie and Elicia quickly rose from their spots and rushed over to the window. As they dove onto the sofa their faces gleamed with the thought of their yard turning into a wonderful blanket of white. With their faces plastered against the window it seemed the snowflakes were eager to meet them. Oh, how they wished they could melt through the glass and join the outside world in the fun.

Seeing her children's noses pressed flat against the window Cassandra decided to cave in to their unspoken pleas. "All right, you may go outside for a little while." The upheaval that followed caused her to add, "But you need to change into some warmer clothes." With that said her children leapt off the sofa and hurried towards their rooms.

By then Sean had stepped right into the path of his children. Quick to react he raised the tray of mugs just in time. As the two disappeared down the hall he slowly lowered the tray. He swiftly assessed the mugs of hot cocoa and was relieved none had spilled. He continued towards the living room. As he entered, he looked over at his wife and asked, "What was that all about?"

He watched as his wife gently pulled back the curtain. And to his surprise it was snowing. With his eyes glued to the wonderful site, he slowly sat the tray onto the coffee table. Then unexpectedly it hit him, "Oh I get it. You told the kids they could go outside." When he glanced down at his wife the twinkle in her eye, along with her soft smile, gave him his answer. Then as she reached over and cupped her hands around one of the mugs he added, "And you want me to go with them."

Cassandra didn't have to say a word. She just watched as her husband walked away then disappeared down the hallway. With the living room now all to herself she leaned back against the sofa and took a sip from her cocoa. She savored the warmth as it ran down her throat. And when it reached the pit of her stomach, she let out a pleasing sigh. Now, ready to relax, she collected the quilt from the back of the sofa and covered her lap. She snuggled once more into the corner, and after retrieving her book from under the quilt she opened it to the marked page.

She quickly submerged herself into the world of pirates, and before long she imagined herself as the heroin, disguised as a young sailor, scrambling on her knees while chasing after a scrub brush. It seemed the others found great pleasure in playing keep away and laughed heartedly at her plight. They continued to kick the scrub brush out of reach until finally had come to rest in front of a pair of black boots. When all went quiet, she glanced up. Standing above her was a tall man dressed in dark clothing staring down at her with yellowish-green eyes. Fear slowly grew within her. While her throat began to close, she heard a loud Crackle, crackle, pop!

Suddenly she was drawn towards the fireplace and the mantle where the Christmas garland hung. The deep green holly leaves and bright red berries made a nice back drop for the stockings that hung down from the mantle. Then without warning her quiet warm thoughts were replaced by two gleeful screeches and one mild tone chuckle. She turned her attention towards them just in time to find her husband trying to zip up Elicia's coat without success. Knowing she was the only one who knew how to fix it she called her over.

"Hurry! They're going to beat me outside and throw snowballs at me," begged Elicia.

"Now, now," Cassandra stated as she waited for her daughter to stretch out her arms, "your father wouldn't do that to you." With her daughter now in position she pulled the zippers teeth close together as she tugged upward.

"No, but Ronnie would." Elicia then pushed out her bottom lip as if she was about to pout.

"There, you're all set." When Cassandra caught a glimpse of the protruding lip, she tapped her cheek and requested, "Now make use of that thing and give me a kiss."

Elicia leaned forward and gave her mother what she wanted. But there was something she wanted in return. "Please come outside with us."

As Elicia stood in front of her, Cassandra couldn't help but be struck by her big round blue eyes. They twinkled with such excitement that there was no way she could say no. So, after she sent Elicia to join the others, she flipped off the blanket and headed towards her bedroom.

When she entered her bedroom she went straight towards the walk-in closet, flipped on the light then headed toward the section where she kept her old garments from years past. There she found her white and purple snow pants. She quickly snagged them off the hanger then left. After reaching her side of the bed she plopped down, pulled the snowsuit over her pajama pants, stood up then shuffled them up the rest of the way. As she pulled the straps over her shoulders she thought, "so far so good." Now for the final test she lay down on the bed and zipped. Relieved the snow pants still fit she got up and hurried to join her family in the winter fun.

Even though it was evening the snow gave off the illusion of midday. As Cassandra stepped outside, she was welcomed by the peacefulness of it all. For a moment she savored it then went in search of her family. She followed the footprints that lead to the back yard. And there is where she found the two men of her life packing snow into blocks. But there was no sign of her daughter. As she glanced around the yard, she finally spotted her lying in the snow. Carefully she made her way towards her.

Elicia was still swishing her arms and legs when she spotted her mom. Thrilled, she stopped then reached up and grabbed hold of her outstretched hand. After her mom helped her back to her feet she stated, "Look, I made lots of angels to protect us." She then pointed towards the indents in the snow.

Cassandra's eyes followed her daughter's finger, and from the looks of it she had indeed been terribly busy with her mission. From where she stood, she saw at least seven. Seven being her lucky number, she briefly closed her eyes and prayed for more snow. It seemed to work because the snowflakes had become larger. With a smile she looked back down at her daughter and saw the disappointment on her face. She glanced over to where her daughter was looking and realized she wanted to be part of their fun. Wanting to bring the gleam back, she knelt and gathered up some snow. As she packed it into a small ball she asked, "Elicia, would you like to help me build a snowman?" When her daughter's eyes widened, she had her answer. She handed the ball to her and together they rolled it to collect more snow.

Across the yard Sean smiled as he watched his wife helping their little girl build their own winter creation. He had tried to get her involved with building the fort, but she had her mind set on making snow angels for her mother. He watched the two as they packed and rolled the snowball across the yard until suddenly a slight sting struck the left side of his face followed by a slow cold wet drip. As he turned to see where the object had come from, he was hit once more in the chest. Then he spotted his son barricaded behind their half-built fort and forming another snowball. With no time to waste he leaned over and grabbed a handful of the white powder. He quickly formed it then threw it in the direction of the new incoming bomb.

"You missed," Ronnie shouted as the snowball splattered just short of the fort. He then remembered his dad's pitching arm and soon realized he might not be so lucky with the next. He scrambled to collect a large amount of snow and packed it. After quickly discarding that one he continued to make more. One after another he hurled the snowballs towards his dad. And to his surprise more of them hit their target than not.

Impressed by his son's aim Sean stopped gathering snow and decided to hide behind one of the trees in the yard. He ran as fast as he could towards the biggest and oldest. And when he was safe behind it, he had time to catch his breath. As he rested against the tree, he quickly devised a plan to outwit his son.

Meanwhile, Cassandra was in the middle of helping her daughter lift the snowman's middle when she caught a glimpse of two figures running across the yard. She swiftly packed it into place then gave the others her undivided attention. She watched the two trample through the ever-deepening snow, trying to beat the other to their incomplete winter fortress. Holding back her laughter she glanced back down at her daughter and asked, "Elicia, who do you think will win the race?" She could tell the wheels were turning in Elicia's head as if she was calculating the distance and speed of both contestants.

"Mommy," Elicia finally said as she looked up, "don't get mad, but I think Ronnie will win."

"Why do you say that honey?" Just then Cassandra looked over to see her husband trip and fall flat into the snow.

"That's why mommy. Daddy's feet are too big, and his bootlaces always come undone."

The two giggled softly then went back to packing the snow needed to start the head of their snowman. They rolled the ball a little way then stopped to pack it then rolled it some more. When it was the right size Cassandra lifted her daughter up to carefully place the smaller ball on top of the body. "There," she said as she lowered her daughter to the ground, "it's done."

"No, it's not," Elicia stated.

"What do you mean? We have a head, body and a bottom. It is now complete." Cassandra knew what her little girl meant, but she wanted her to feel important and to make this snowman her own.

"Don't be silly. We need eyes so he can see all the beautiful Christmas decorations."

Agreeing with her daughter she took her hand and led her back to the house.

Upon entering the warmth of their home Cassandra, along with Elicia wiped their boots on the mat before she closed the door. Then almost in unison they quickly discarded their gloves, coats and boots. When they had completely rid themselves of everything wet Cassandra directed her daughter to wait for her in the living room then slipped around the corner into the hallway.

While waiting for her mother's return Elicia fidgeted on the sofa. She had been unable to bottle up her delight about the snow, so she decided to look out the window. She pulled back the curtains, and to her amazement the falling snow had almost completely covered the tracks they had just made moments ago. Wanting to know how things were going with her brother she looked farther out into the yard. When she spotted him, it had come as no surprise that her father was still trying to coax him out of the fort. Along with a grin she shook her head then whispered, "Give it up dad. You will never win with Ronnie."

"Who won't win?" asked Cassandra as she placed the long plastic box down on the coffee table. When her daughter didn't answer she shrugged her shoulders then opened the lid to the box. "Look sweetie, I found my box of buttons. I'm sure we could find some eyes for your snowman in here."

After releasing the curtains Elicia turned away from the window and slid down next to her mother. She took her time eyeing the eight compartments full of assorted sizes and colored buttons. When her eyes narrowed in on one particular button, she used her finger to move the others out of the way. It was a large deep royal blue button simply perfect for the snowman's eyes. As she picked it up, she said, "Mom this is what I want. Can you help me find another just like this one?"

"I'll try, but I can't guarantee that any of these buttons have matches."

"I know this one does. It just has to."

One glance into her daughter's eyes and Cassandra knew she just had to find a match. She started taking out the buttons from the compartment one at a time. When she reached the bottom, her heart sank. Then before she could form the words that would break her daughter's heart, one of her fingers just happened to rest upon the one she was looking for.

"See, I told you there was a match," stated Elicia as she looked up at her mother.

"Yes, you did. Now let's get our coats and boots back on so we can give your snowman his eyes."

"Mommy we can't go outside yet! He still needs to have a nose so he can smell all the good things you will be cooking for Christmas."

"Oh, you're right." Cassandra got up from the sofa and took her daughter by the hand. She led her into the kitchen and when they reached the refrigerator she asked, "So, what do you think will make a good nose for your snowman?" While her daughter thought about the answer, she opened the refrigerator then leaned over and pulled out the vegetable drawer. Right on top she spotted a bundle of fresh broccoli and pulled it out, "how about this?"

As her mother held up the broccoli Elicia crinkled up her nose. "No, that's too green and bumpy."

"Okay," Cassandra swiftly traded it for a bag of freshly picked green beans, "how about this?"

"Now you're just being silly," stated Elicia. Disappointed in her mother's choices she moved in closer then leaned over to look for herself. Soon her eyes spotted exactly what she was looking for, "There, that carrot."

"This one," Cassandra asked as she pulled out the one carrot that was long and straight.

Elicia just smiled then snatched the carrot out of her mother's hand and placed it with the buttons she was holding.

After closing the refrigerator Cassandra decided to ask one last question, "Anything else before going back outside?"

Taking her finger and tapping it on her nose, Elicia rolled her eyes up as if the question needed some serious thought. After a few seconds she stopped tapping and slowly lowered her hand. "How about some...umm... red licorice for his mouth? That way whatever he eats will taste sweet." With her mother in agreement, she felt a sense of pride. And she hoped there would be extras to eat. As her mother went to gather the licorice, she was sent off to get ready. Back in the entryway she placed the snowman's eyes and nose down on the cedar bench then sat alongside them. After she managed to pull her pink snow boots on by herself, she grabbed her coat. And just like earlier she put it on then waited for her mother to zip her up.

After both were bundled Cassandra opened the front door and on the other side stood her husband, covered from head to foot with snow,

Cassandra allowed a slight giggle to escape. As he shook himself off, she asked, "What in God's name happened to you?"

Sean only grumbled as he entered the house.

"Don't tell me Ronnie has out witted you in a snowball fight?" asked Cassandra. By the look on his face, she could tell she was right. She then raised her hand to cover the grin that was widening.

"Boy, I didn't know that kid could run so fast in the snow." Sean took off his cap and leaned over to give his wife a kiss on the cheek. "I only came back to recharge myself with a little snack. And hopefully find something I can use to call a truce with your son."

Barely able to contain herself, Elicia finally burst out laughing. But when she realized her father was glaring at her she calmed down and offered him some advice, "Daddy maybe you should give him some licorice. That way he would be busy concentrating on chewing instead of throwing."

"You really think that would work, little angel?"

"Oh yes daddy. Mommy always says boys are simple minded and can only concentrate on one thing at a time."

Sean raised his brow then slowly moved his gaze from his daughter towards his wife, "Oh...really?"

"Yes daddy."

Cassandra recognized that glare and knew she was in trouble. To avoid confrontation, she grabbed Elicia by the arm, scurried her outside then slammed the door. With an obstacle now in the way she gave them more time to escape. She led them down the stairs and when they reached the ground, she heard the front door fly open. Without turning around, she exchanged her daughter's arm for her hand. "Run!" she shouted as she yanked her daughter in the direction of the snow fort.

Not understanding what was going on, Elicia asked while catching her breath, "Mommy, why is daddy chasing us?"

"No time. We need to reach your brother." As soon as Cassandra finished, she felt a strong downward pull. When she glanced behind her she saw Elicia lying in the snow. Quickly she collected her under her arm, and like a football she carried her across the backyard. The extra weight and the rising snow slowed her down. But when they finally reached the fortress, she lowered Elicia to the ground then asked her son, "Can we borrow your fort?"

Eyeing the red licorice in his mother's hand Ronnie answered, "It's going to cost you," then pointed at the long red candy.

"Okay, but only two pieces. The rest is for your sister's snowman." Cassandra then noticed her husband was getting closer. "Ronnie can we also use some of your snowballs?"

Ronnie stood quietly as he held out his hand waiting for his payment.

"Oh yah...sorry," Cassandra quickly handed him his pieces of licorice then stuffed the rest into her pocket. Then as soon as her hands were empty, she picked up one of the pre-made snowballs from the pile and threw it as hard as she could towards her husband. Unfortunately, it barely fazed him as it brushed his right shoulder. In a panic she turned to her daughter, "Elicia grab a snowball and help me hit your father."

"Why?"

"Don't ask questions, just throw."

Hoping her father wouldn't get mad, Elicia did as her mother requested and picked up a snowball. But when she went to throw it, she realized she put on the wrong gloves. Part of the snow had stuck to her mittens while some of it plopped to the ground. Before she had the time to get upset her brother held out a pair of gloves. Gratefully she looked up and almost laughed.

"They will help you throw better," Ronnie muttered through the licorice clinched between his teeth.

While their mother kept the assault going, Elicia hurried and took off her mittens. She handed them to Ronnie in exchange for his gloves. After slipping them on Ronnie planted a snowball into her hands then slyly grinned and motioned his head towards their mom. With a giggle and a nod Elicia agreed.

After gathering a snowball for himself Ronnie yelled, "Now!" Together they threw their weapons at their mother. And when they hit their target Ronnie claimed, "See those gloves work."

Cassandra felt betrayed as the splattered snow slid down her coat. And because of it she diverted her attention towards her children. Within that split second Sean took the advantage and tackled her. Down they went and when they hit the ground Ronnie and Elicia bombarded them with snowballs.

The fun had only come to its end when there were no snowballs left, and their parents were able to sit up. At least they were smiling while they brushed the white power off. With no fear of repercussion Ronnie offered a hand to his mother.

Elicia followed her brother's lead, and as she helped pull up her father she asked, "Now, will someone tell me why daddy was chasing us?" This time she wanted an answer.

"Yes, dear would you like to explain to my daughter why I was chasing her?" Sean sarcastically remarked as he stood up then leaned over to finish brushing off his pants.

Cassandra looked at her husband defiantly then reached out to grab her daughter's hand. "Come on honey lets go finish your snowman before the snowfall covers him."

Unhappy with the response, Elicia snubbed her mother then turned towards her brother and asked, "Will you help me finish my snowman, Ronnie?"

Untraditional

Cassandra had gone back inside with her husband. And once they shed their winter coats they went in different directions. Cassandra headed into the living room so she could keep an eye on her children. After she planted herself on the sofa, she pulled back the curtains, and as she looked out back for her children a gust of wind cloaked her view with a flurry of snow. It was amazing in its beauty, but it didn't last long. Soon she was able to see her children and they were placing the last detail on the snowman. Knowing they would be coming in shortly she got up to collect some towels.

As she made her way down the hall she heard the soft whisper of her name. Believing it be her husband playing a practical joke she turned to scorn him. But when she found the hallway empty the hairs on the back of her neck rose. Suddenly chilled, she rubbed her arms then the sound of the microwave reminded her of her task.

She entered the bathroom just as the wind howled. Its loud echo made Cassandra realize that must have been what she had heard. No longer unnerved she went straight to the linen cabinet, grabbed out a couple of towels, and headed back out to meet her children.

Cassandra reached the front entryway and was surprised her children weren't inside yet. Concerned, she placed the towels on the wooden bench then turned for the door. But before she could open it her husband had come up behind her.

"I'm ready when you are." Sean stood with a tray of re-heated hot chocolate.

"Great," Cassandra turned to him, "just let me call in the kids." She gave him a peck on the cheek then went to open the door. As she twisted the knob a strong gust of wind pushed it wide open. And while the chilly air from outside entered she wrapped her arms around herself. She stepped into the doorway and as she gazed outside, she could barely see past the front porch light.

The wind blew the snow like a solid sheet of white, making it virtually impossible to see her children. Hoping they could hear her she cupped her hands around her mouth like a bull horn and called out, "Kids it's time to come in." For a moment she stood and listened for a reply, but all she received was the whipping sounds of the wind. Her concern soon turned into worry, and when she turned towards her husband for help, she found he had already vanished into the living room.

*Once again Sean deposited the tray of hot chocolate onto the coffee table, knowing this time his children would drink them. While the drinks sat waiting to warm up their owners Sean took the time to wander over to the fireplace. He watched as the flames slowly dimmed with time, so he leaned over and removed the fireplace screen from its resting place. He lifted the screen slightly off the floor and moved it over to the side. With the screen out of the way he knelt in front of the fire. He then grabbed the poker from the fireplace set and began to stroke the fire. As the sparks floated upward, he kept the thought of his children being hammered by the snow in the forefront of his mind. After placing the poker back, he raised his hands up in front of the fire. Not feeling enough heat, he reached over to his left and grabbed one of the logs from the pile. Just as he was about to place it on the fire, he heard some giggles and turned his head towards the entryway. Relief swept over him when he saw his children waiting as his wife helped them take off their winter coats and handed them each a towel.

When her children finished drying off what was not covered by their clothing Cassandra took their towels and temporarily hung them up on one of the empty hooks next to the coats. By the time she turned back her children were sitting on the bench with their legs stretched out waiting for her to help them take off their boots. With a slight grin she knelt in front of them then started with the oldest. After trading their snow boots for warm slippers, she stood back up and ushered them off towards their bedrooms. When the last one disappeared, she grabbed one of the towels from the coat rack and quickly wiped up the water from the floor. She then replaced the towel upon the hook before heading into the living room. Upon spotting her husband kneeling in front of the fireplace she said, "There now, they should be out in a couple of minutes. Do you have everything ready?"

Sean glanced over at his wife to acknowledge her presence then went back to building up the fire. He knew what she was referring to and he was just about ready to read his children a Christmas story when they came out from their rooms. As he poked and stirred the fire, he thought about how the two would sit beside him on the sofa listening intensely to every word while they sipped on their hot coco with marshmallows and whipped cream on top. Just then he remembered what he forgot. He poked at the fire one last time. After placing the poker back with the set, he stood up then put the screen back into place. When he finally looked back over at his wife she was just about to sit down in her recliner.

"Honey, I forgot the mini marshmallows. Could you get them before the kids come out?"

With her knees bent and her hands placed on the arms of the recliner Cassandra sighed. She had been looking forward to relaxing ever since she was interrupted earlier. Yet, she stood back up once she reminded herself the night was not about her, but the children. As she watched her husband make his way over to the sofa then sit down, she replied, "Sure."

Even though she was frustrated with her husband she knew he had also done a lot getting ready for Christmas. So, she walked into the kitchen and straight towards the cabinet where they kept the coffee cups, tea, hot chocolate and more. After opening the door, she stood on the balls of her feet to see the second shelf better. At first, she did not see the mini marshmallows. As she rummaged through the shelf she yelled to her husband, "Honey, I don't see any... Oh wait... nope these are the wrong size. Sorry it looks like we are out. What now?" She was waiting for a response when she heard the children come running out of their rooms. Knowing they would be disappointed she pulled out the bag of regular sized marshmallows. With a new idea in her head, she walked over and opened the counter drawer next to the stove. She quickly grabbed four skewers then closed the drawer.

Ronnie and Elicia sat on the sofa waiting patiently as they watched their father squirt the whip cream onto the top of their hot chocolate. Just as their father was about to top the last cup off Ronnie realized there was something missing and spoke out, "Dad you are not trying to cheat us, are you?" He carefully eyed his father as he waited for his answer.

The look he received from his children made Sean squirmed like a little kid as he tried to find the right words for his lie. Then they let him know they were getting impatient by crossing their arms in front of them. Tiny beads of sweat were beginning to form above his brows when his wife finally entered the room and to his rescue.

"Does anyone want to roast marshmallows in the fireplace?"

Still pouting about the missing mini-marshmallow Elicia answered, "Mom that's not part of our tradition."

Noticing the disappointment in her daughter's tone Cassandra laid out the skewers on top of the coffee table along with the bag of marshmallows. She then looked over at her and replied, "Sweetie, that's the nice thing about traditions. It's okay if once and a while you must change it. Nothing is set in stone." As she continued to investigate her children's faces, she began to feel guilty things were not going as planned. To take the blame and disapproving eyes off herself she decided to blurt out, "Okay, your father forgot the marshmallows."

"Thanks honey," said Sean as he got up. He then walked around the table until he was behind his wife. As he grabbed his wife by her hips he continued, "I always wanted to be the bad guy."

Suddenly Cassandra was yanked towards the floor. As she fell backwards, she tried to grab hold of the coffee table, but it was too late. When she stopped, she ended up on top of her husband. Deciding not to give up without a fight she began to twist her body around until she was facing him. Now looking into his eyes, she placed a hand on each side of him. As he smiled back at her she waited until he raised his hands to brush her hair away from her face before making her move. With his waist unprotected she shifted all her weight from her arms onto his body. She then slowly moved her hands up to his sides so not to alarm him. When she found the right spot, she lightly used her fingertips to tickle his sides. However, it didn't take long for her to realize she had miscalculated. The next thing she knew her husband began tickling her back. Being more sensitive to the touch she automatically withdrew her hands from his sides and tried to protect her own body. Unsuccessful in her defense she broke out in laughter as she squirmed.

Standing over the coffee table Ronnie and Elicia watched as their parents' reversed positions during their playful fight. After a while it had become embarrassing to watch, and they knew they had to stop it. The two whispered back and forth until they had a clever idea. As Ronnie walked over and stood on one side of their parents his sister went to the other. When they were in place, the two of them carefully plopped on top of their parents then joined in on the fun.

What started out as one large pile of bodies quickly split into two as each parent got the upper hand and chose a child to tickle. Cassandra rolled and laughed along with her daughter across the floor as they slowly moved away from the boys. They all seemed to be having a wonderful time until her daughter cried out.

"Stop, I can't breathe."

Being on the bottom Cassandra released her daughter and helped her roll over onto the floor. Concerned about her asthma, she listened to her breathing patterns. Unable to tell she finally asked, "Are you okay sweetie? Do you need your inhaler?"

"No Mommy, but my sides hurt. I think I laughed too much." Elicia rolled onto her side then slowly pushed herself up to sit. She took a few minutes to rest while she watched everyone else grab a skewer to move on to the next thing. As she sat alone, she lowered her head and began twisting the corner of her pajama shirt between her fingers. She felt bad about breaking up the fun, but before she had a chance to cry about it her brother walked up and stood in front of her. As she looked up, he smiled and held out a skewer holding three marshmallows. Relieved he wasn't mad at her she returned his smile then took the skewer. With help she got to her feet and together they walked towards the fireplace to join their parents.

With their children now by their sides Sean stated, "Now kids, remember not to get too close to the fire. If you need help don't be afraid to ask one of us." Before opening the screen, he glanced over his shoulder. When he saw the concern on his wife's face, he added, "Stand here at the edge of the tile floor and do not lean over. Your skewers should be long enough to reach."

As her husband opened the fireplace screen Cassandra cringed slightly at the thought of one of her children catching on fire. "Maybe this was a bad idea," she voiced while she watched her children step closer to the flames.

"No mommers, it's a great idea," Ronnie snapped back for he loved his mother because she always came up with creative and new things to do. Plus, this was the first time they would be allowed to enjoy the fire close without going camping. However, he began to rethink his outburst and soon retracted it. "Maybe you're right mom." When his mother gave him a puzzled look, he smiled and said, "I believe this idea could be better if we made smores with our roasted marshmallows."

"Ronners, I do believe you are right," Cassandra said with a grin. Leave it to her son to make an idea even better. "What do you two say? Should we have smores?"

"Yes, Oh yes," let out Elicia as she jumped up and down. By now she was no longer thinking about untraditional their Christmas Eve was turning out to be.

"Well, the two of you will have to find a way to per sway your father. After all, this is his time with you." As the last word came out of her mouth her children rushed up towards her and handed her their skewers with partially roasted marshmallows.

The two wasted no time running over to their father. Elicia took it upon herself to claim her father's lap and hug him as tight as she could, while Ronnie went behind him and wrapped his arms around his neck. The two did not let go, as they pleaded repeatedly.

If the sounds of a broken record screaming in his ear wasn't enough to make him cave, then the constriction of his lungs and airway were. Finally, Sean had no other choice and answered, "Ok...ok...ok."

When she had the answer she wanted, Cassandra walked over and waited for her children to release their father. After handing them back their skewers she headed into the kitchen to gather the chocolate bars and gram crackers. She entered the pantry and found the gram crackers on one shelf while the chocolate bars were mixed in with the left-over candy from Halloween. Once she had what she was looking for tucked in her arm she closed the pantry door and began humming her favorite Christmas tune. It was turning out to be the best Christmas Eve ever with the snow still falling and roasting marshmallows by the fire. Now, all that was left was a delightful story to help the mood continue.

When she entered back into the living room she paused and leaned up against the wall. The sight of her husband knelt in front of the fire helping their children blow out the flames on their marshmallows gave her a sense of warmth. She continued to stand quietly hoping not to bring attention to her for she wanted to savor the moment. Finally, she glanced down at her watch and realized they were gravely behind schedule. She whistled to catch her husband's attention then pointed at her watch. With a nod of his head, she continued into the room. "Okay, kids it's time for your father to read 'How The Grinch Stole Christmas', so grab your chocolate bars and gram crackers and take your seats."

As the kids hurried to do what their mother said, Sean stood up and went about closing the fireplace screen before walking over to the bookcase. This was his favorite part of the holiday season since having their children. And being the storyteller made it even that much better. He knew most families traditionally read "The Night Before Christmas", but for some reason a few years back he just felt a different classic by Dr. Seuss would do the job just as well. And for the most part the story had proven him right. He smiled to himself as he reached up to grab the book but stopped short of pulling it completely out when he felt a tug on his shirt. He then turned his head to see the face of their smallest child with her big blue eyes staring up at him.

With her father now looking down at her, Elicia allowed her smile to grow. When he smiled back, she slowly brought her hand around the front and held up the DVD she had in her hand. She then asked, "Daddy is it alright if we watch the movie instead of you reading the book tonight?"

Sean watched as his daughter swayed back and forth fluttering her long dark eyelashes at him. He recognized that look all too well and knew the idea had not come from her, or at least not entirely. Somewhat disappointed he slid the book back into its spot then leaned over and took the movie from his daughter's hand. With her now happy he made his way over to the DVD player while his daughter ran over to the sofa. Before kneeling in front of the DVD player he thought he would try one last time to plead with his children to read the book. But by the time he glanced over he changed his mind when he saw the chocolate smiles on their faces as they scooted into their places. He shook his head in disbelief then motioned for his wife to clean them up before he joined them. With a light chuckle he watched his children squirm while his wife tried to wash away their treasured treats. This was indeed turning out to be an untraditional Christmas Eve. Even so he planned to make the best of it, so he turned back to the DVD player, knelt and put the movie in. As the movie was loading, he got up and on his way towards the sofa he grabbed the remote from the coffee table. With everything now in place, he snuggled down between his son and daughter.

After throwing the used tissues into the fireplace Cassandra grabbed the blanket from the back of the recliner and sat down. As she raised the footrest she leaned back and took a mental picture of her family sitting across from her all snuggled together under one big quilt. She smiled to herself while watching her husband finish eating his smores while their children sipped on their hot chocolate. The only thing left out of this perfect picture was her. However, it was perfect, nonetheless. She continued to take in the moment as her husband brought their two small heads under his arms and snuggled them in closer to his body. This was his time with the children, even though he was not reading the story. With that in mind she reached over to the end table and cupped her hands around her cup of hot cocoa. As she sat back up, she brought the cup to her lips then took a sip. She closed her eyes and sighed as the warmth ran down the back of her throat and into her stomach. It always amazed her how a sip of hot chocolate could make her feel so warm and peaceful inside. When the sensation stopped, she reopened her eyes.

Sensing his wife's stare Sean looked over at her and noticed she was glancing behind him. Turning his head he gazed through the slight brake between the curtains and understood what was on her mind. He then turned his head back to her and smiled gently as he pulled the two bundles of joy closer to his sides. Tonight was going to be a chilly one. But if he had anything to do with it, he would make sure the inside would stay warm. As if they could read his thoughts his children laid their heads upon his chest letting him know they fully trusted him in keeping them safe.

Comfortable under her father's left arm Elicia quietly watched her favorite Christmas show until it came to one particular spot. She raised her head slightly and stated, "Oh! This is my favorite part." She then pointed to the TV as the Grinch stood in the snow leaning against his cave with a devious grin while the fir on top of his head curled then slowly rolled its way out straight when he had an awful idea.

"I can see why," Sean stated as he looked down at his daughter. "He looks like you right before you do something that gets you into trouble."

From across the room Cassandra watched as her daughter took her hand out of the quilt and smacked her father in the chest. She quietly giggled to herself for she knew her husband was right. Their daughter did have a particularly devious look when she was up to something she knew was wrong but wanted to do it anyway. Then in a few short seconds it seemed all was forgiven when her daughter looked up at her father as he tightened his arm around her, and she smiled. As she raised her cup back up to her lips, she continued to lovingly watch her family. It was times like this one she realized she had everything she had ever wanted, a husband who not only loved her but their children. And a boy, and girl who brought so much joy and laughter into their household. With happiness in her heart, she shifted her gaze towards the warm glow of the fireplace and to where the four stockings hung upon the mantel waiting to be filled with the small gifts from Santa.

The first one was more traditional because it was long and red with a white furry cuff upon the top which belonged to her husband. The next in line was almost the very opposite of the previous for it was smaller in length and white with a red felt cuff. But the white stocking had one more detail to it. In the center carefully placed sat a puppy wearing a Santa hat on its head and a blue wrapped gift with a red bow hanging out of its mouth. Indeed, this one truly belonged to her son since he had a powerful desire and passion to care for all living creatures. As her eyes made their way to the third stocking her smile widened. There hung the oddball stocking her little girl had picked out for herself. It definitely stood out from the rest with its deep crushed green velvet and green, red and black plaid cuff cut with points that hung down. Tied at each point were golden jingle bells that sounded as sweet as her daughter's voice when they bounced. At last, her eyes fell upon the one stocking at the end, and she sighed. This one was special to her heart because her children had picked it out for her while shopping with their father. The light blue knitted stocking had a cuff made of white to make it look like snow covering the winter scene below. And as she focused harder on the image in the middle, she realized the snowman was identical to the one her and her daughter had just made in the front yard. With a deeper sense of warmth, she settled back into her chair and took another sip from her mug.

Butterfly Kisses

As the credits rolled at the end of the movie Sean removed his arms from around his children. He then grabbed a hold of the quilt as he announced it was time for them to go to bed. The moans and disappointing pouts soon followed but he ignored them as he folded up the quilt then re-draped it over the back of the sofa. When he was done, he turned back around only to have his children quickly wrapped their arms around his waist. Not able to lower his arms he tried to reason with them, but to no avail. Left with no other choice he dug his hands in between his body and his children's arms then pushed outwards. Instead of prying their arms off of him like he had hoped it only forced his children to clamp onto his upper arms. Understanding what they wanted him to do and not wanting to spoil their fun he allowed them to grab tighter to his upper arms. He then raised them up slowly to make sure their hands would not slide off.

From her recliner Cassandra watched her husband walk across the floor as their children hung on trying not to fall to the floor. She took note of his direction and was pleased he was heading towards the hallway. But before he got there, he stopped then turned his head towards her. She had been caught all snuggled up comfortably while staring at his predicament. Feeling guilty she was about to look away when she found her husband pleading with her for help. He tried to use her own trick, but she could not give him the same results. For some reason, a man fluttering his eyes while pushing out his bottom lip only made her want to laugh.

She sat for a few more seconds hoping he would fix his own mess. When he didn't make the effort to try, she placed her empty mug back on top of the end table then pulled down the lever to retract the footrest. She made her way over towards her husband and decided it would be best to start with her son. Wrapping her left arm around her son's waist she held him up while her right hand pried his fingers from the arm they held hostage. It wasn't an easy task for once she had one finger off, he would find a way to clamp it back on as she moved to another. After awhile she knew she had to use drastic measures. "Ronnie, your father is right. It is already passed your bedtime, and Santa will not come until you are fast asleep."

Ronnie huffed and with a little disappointment in his voice he said, "Ok." He then let go of his father's arm allowing his mother to take his full weight.

After Cassandra lowered her son's feet to the floor, she kissed him on the cheek then patted him on the behind. "Now off to bed with you. I will be in to tuck you in as soon as I un-cling your sister."

Ronnie didn't argue and started to head towards his bedroom. But when he reached the hallway, he stopped. He knew they had forgotten something particularly important, so he looked back just in time to see his mother lowering his sister to the floor. Before she had a chance to scoot his sister off as well, he said, "Mommers!"

Cassandra looked up and over at her son. She was slightly irritated to see he was still standing at the entrance of the hallway. "Shouldn't you be in bed?"

"But mom, we haven't set out the milk and cookies for Santa yet."

Realizing her son was right Cassandra turned her daughter in the direction of the kitchen then waved her son over to join them. "We'll have to make it quick. We can't keep Santa waiting." She then walked out of the living room with her daughter in hand, leaving her husband to clear away their mess. By the time she reached the kitchen her son had already scooted a chair over to the island counter and was hovering over the trays of cookies. She let go of her daughter and told her to stand by her brother until she came back. Once her daughter agreed she went into the dining room to grab another chair.

In a hurry to make up some of the lost time she picked up the nearest chair and brought it back for her daughter to climb on. With both children now able to see the cookies she asked, "Which ones do you two want to leave for Santa?"

Being the oldest Ronnie took it upon himself to answer his mother first. "I want to leave Santa a snicker doodle."

"Are you sure?" asked Cassandra somewhat puzzled. She had never known her son to give up one of his favorites willingly before.

Ronnie thought his mother's question was dumb, so he gave her a queer look. "Yes, I'm sure. Remember I'm eight now I think I'm mature enough to share. Plus, I will choose another in case Santa doesn't like it."

Proud of her son Cassandra smiled. Then while he was busy figuring out his next choice, she turned her attention towards her daughter. "Have you found a cookie for Santa?"

"Well..." Elicia paused for a moment, "If Ronnie is willing to give up one of his favorites, then I will give up one of mine." She looked down at the cookie tray full of ginger snaps and for a brief second, she almost changed her mind. But wanting to prove she could be mature like her brother, she did not.

Now that they had each picked out a cookie Cassandra turned away from them and went over to the cabinets between the sink and the stove to retrieve a small plate to put Santa's snacks on. When she opened the cabinet, she remembered the plate she wanted was on one of the top shelves out of reach. Luckily, her husband had come in and put the dishes he had just cleaned up into the sink. Before he had the chance to leave, she recruited his services. As he stretched up high, she gave him the directions to where she kept the Christmas dishes and had him pull out one of the ceramic plates.

The plate set had been given to her as a Christmas gift last year by her children and would be perfect for this occasion. As her husband handed her the plate, she remembered the pride her children had on their cute little faces when she opened the gift. She then ran her hand over the plate with red trim and a hand painted picture of an old

English style Santa in the middle. When she heard her husband ask if she needed anything else she sighed and shook her head. After her husband left, she turned her attention back towards the task at hand. It was then she noticed her children were in a deep discussion on what other cookies should go on their plate.

"No, this one looks more like Santa," stated Ronnie as he reached across the tray and pointed to one of the Santa face sugar cookies that was decorated with icing.

Elicia followed her brother's finger with her eyes then replied, "Ok, but I want this one." She took her tiny finger and directed it over one of the snowmen.

"Santa doesn't want a cookie that doesn't look like him," huffed Ronnie.

"Yes, he does," Elicia insisted.

"No, he doesn't."

When she saw her mother come up beside her Elicia looked over at her with sad eyes. "Mommy! Tell Ronnie Santa wants a snowman so he can remember his visit to our house."

Before answering her daughter Cassandra placed the plate on the countertop in between her children. She then picked up the cookies they had previously chosen and put them on it. With that done she wrapped an arm around each child and finally asked, "How about a compromise?"

The crinkled-up noses told her neither one wanted to give in to the other. Knowing this tiff was going to put them even further behind schedule she intervened and said, "Ronnie you want the Santa so take it and put it on the plate. And Elicia you do the same with yours."

With them both in agreement she watched as they tried not to get in each other's way while collecting their decorated cookie. Once the cookies were on the plate with the others Cassandra withdrew her arms from around her children and said, "Now that the two of you are done why don't I pick out a cookie for Santa's wife?"

"That is a great idea," Ronnie shouted out. When he looked at his sister for reassurance, he noticed she didn't understand, so he stated, "You still have so much to learn." He then leaned over the counter so he could whisper to her, "Mrs. Claus is the one who makes all the goodies we get in our stockings."

"Oooh...now I see." With a better understanding of how it worked, Elicia hurriedly grabbed her mother's arm and tugged. "Mommy, take your time. No pressure."

"Yeah, no pressure," reinstated Ronnie.

"Well then, as long as there is no pressure I should get on with it," said Cassandra as she carefully glanced down at the trays of sugar cookies.

Although she already knew the one, she raised her hand and slowly moved it across the first cookie tray. As her hand hovered over the cookies, she would casually glance over at her children to see their reaction. Then she let her hand stop briefly over a cookie. When they shook their heads, she knew it was not the one. She continued on the stopped again only to get the same reaction. So far it looked like the bell, the star and ornament were out of the question. Finally, she lowered her hand upon the angel and without waiting for her children's approval she carefully grabbed hold of it with her fingertips and picked it up. "I like this one."

"Good choice." Ronnie smiled at his mother.

"I like it too," added Elicia.

"Good. Then we all agree." Cassandra placed the last cookie on the plate then helped her children down off their chairs. It was now time to head back into the living room.

Sean had just finished cleaning off the TV tray next to his recliner for Santa's treats when his wife and children entered. "Ah...perfect timing."

As he squatted down and held out his arms his children rushed towards him in excitement. The force as the two plowed into his arms made him close his eyes and almost knocked him over. However, he had managed to brace himself well enough to just sway a little. When he reopened his eyes, he hugged his children tighter. Then his gaze fell past them and towards his wife. She looked so beautiful in her blue flannel pajama bottoms with white snowflakes, especially while bent over carefully rearranging the cookies on the plate. His eyes were then drawn upward as she raised her hand to move the hair from her face and delicately placed it behind her ear with her finger. As if to notice his stare his wife turned her head briefly and smiled before returning back to the cookies. What a lucky man he was to have a beautiful wife who had given him two wonderful and just as beautiful children. Then as if on cue, both children slightly pushed away and looked down at him.

"Dad, will you write our letter to Santa?" Ronnie asked then remembered what had happened the year before when he had asked that very same question. "And this time ask Santa to draw a better picture of Rudolph."

"Yeah, daddy we don't want just the head," Elicia reminded her father.

Sean glanced over at his wife who had been extremely quiet up to this point. She stood in the background with her hand covering her mouth as if trying not to laugh. Ignoring her jester, he looked back at his children and said, "I'll tell you what. Get me a piece of paper and something to write with. Both of you can help me write the note while your mother gets a glass of milk for Santa."

Without hesitation Ronnie and Elicia dashed towards their playroom in search of the items they needed. When they reached the doorway Ronnie reached around the corner and flicked on the light switch so his sister would trip on anything when they walked. Able to see, the two made their way over to the old wooden school desk their father said he had found at a garage sale. For some reason Ronnie didn't believe him. He had always thought the beat-up old desk belonged to his father as a little boy. Now it belonged to them. As they approached, he stood back and waited for his sister to climb onto the seat before lifting the top to the desk.

As her brother held open the desktop Elicia quickly rummaged around to find a blank piece of paper. When she found one, she moved her hands out of the way so her brother could claim one of the pencils from the hand carved built in pencil holder. With the items they needed in hand Ronnie closed the desktop and the two hurried back out into the living room.

"Here Dad!" the two exclaimed as they ran straight towards their father's recliner with pencil and paper held out in front of them.

"Ok. Now, we have to do this quickly. Your mother is grumbling about the time," Sean informed them as he looked over at his wife who was glaring as she pointed to her watch.

Ronnie turned his head towards his sister and when she nodded her head, he knew they both agreed. He turned his head back towards his dad and said, "Dad why don't you write the letter for us so that mom can tuck us into bed."

"Sounds like a plan." Sean took the paper and pencil from his children then leaned back in his recliner. He sat there pondering what he was going to put into this especially important letter to Santa, while his wife took over with their children.

Cassandra waited for her children as she turned her back and stretched out both arms with opened palms facing them. When she felt their hands squeeze around hers the three of them walked down the hall. Their first stop would be the room to their right. With this one belonging to her son, she let go of her daughter's hand and asked her to wait in the hall. As they entered the room, Ronnie quickly let go of her hand and dashed towards his bed. She tried to hurry behind him, but he had already taken flight allowing himself to bounce once then plop on top of the covers. "Now Ronnie..." she said when she reached the bed and leaned over to pull back his covers, "you know you are not to bounce on your bed."

"I know," Ronnie answered as he lifted his knees closer to his upper body in order to allow his mother to slide the comforter and sheets out from underneath him. Then he looked at her with his big blue eyes and added, "But you have already forgiven me because I am so darn cute."

"Unfortunately, I will have to agree with you. But only this time young man." Cassandra waited until her son slid his feet inside and turned over to face her before covering him up. She then tucked the comforter in around him. When he was all snuggled in, she leaned closer and placed a kiss on his cheek then whispered, "Good night little man."

"Good night mom," Ronnie whispered back. He then allowed his head to sink down into his pillow as his mother stood up. Just as he was about to close his eyes, he remembered something and shouted, "Hey! Where is my noozle?"

In her haste to make up time Cassandra had forgotten the most important part of tucking her son into bed. She turned around and walked back. Once beside him she knelt down. No words of apologies were needed as she leaned over and with her nose she lightly brushed against his. Together they quickly rubbed their noses back and forth a few times. When they were done, she pulled her nose away from his and was about to get up when unexpectedly her son wrapped his arms around her neck and gave her a big hug. "I love you too," she whispered then gave him one more kiss on the cheek. When she was done, she stood back up and headed towards the door. She was about halfway to the door when she paused and turned to remind him, "Now don't forget to say your prayers."

"Yes, Mommers," answered Ronnie as he watched his mother take a hold of his sister's hand and disappear.

Finally, inside her daughter's room Cassandra waited as her daughter climbed up onto her bed and curled her legs onto her pillow.

When her daughter was ready, she lifted the covers and held them up until her body slid beneath them. After lowering the cover, she tucked her in tight. She then sat down next to her with one leg on the bed and the other touching the floor. Now in position she leaned over to give her daughter a kiss.

Before her mother could place the kiss on her cheek Elicia asked, "Mommy, why do you give me butterfly kisses and Ronnie noozles?"

Taken by surprise by her daughter's question, Cassandra sat back up. She had always told them there were no favorites in her eyes. But now her daughter's question made it sound as if she did. How could she defuse the unspoken question stirring in her daughter's head? She had to come up with a good answer and quick. "Well sweetie, your brother's nose is more ticklish just like your cheek." When her daughter said nothing, she realized she was hoping for something more, so she added, "Plus butterfly kisses are special."

"How come?"

"Well, my mother, your grandmother used to give me butterfly kisses when I was a little girl."

"Really?" Elicia's eyes lit up at the thought.

"Yes. Really." Cassandra then placed an arm across her daughter. As she leaned in closer, she stated, "You know butterfly kisses are supposed to represent angels."

"They do?"

"Yes. They say when someone's eye lash flutters on your cheek its like having an angel's wing blessing you."

"Ok, I guess I will keep the butterfly kisses." Elicia then snuggled in tighter wearing a smile upon her face.

"I'm glad." Cassandra lowered herself back down closer to her daughter's face. As soon as her right eyelash brushed close to her daughter's cheek she asked, "Are you ready?"

"Yes mommy." Elicia giggled with delight.

"Ok, here we go." Cassandra began to rapidly close and open her eyes. After a few seconds she stopped with her eyes still closed. When she finally reopened them, she pushed herself back up. She continued to sit beside her daughter to watch as her smile turned into contentment. Just when she thought she was going to sleep she whispered, "Good night sweetheart."

Feeling her mother about to move Elicia asked, "Mom?"

"Yes."

Before finishing her question Elicia paused. She didn't want to upset her mother by putting them further behind schedule, but this was the only perfect time to ask, "Can I give you a butterfly kiss?"

"Sure," she replied without hesitation. Cassandra then leaned back down and allowed her daughter to grab hold of her face. As her daughter began the fluttering of her eyes, she slowly closed her own.

The soft gentle brushes across her cheek took her back to when she was a little girl and soon, she could feel her mother's fingers running through her hair. A tingling sensation ran down her spine with every stroke making her more comfortable and ready to sleep. When the combing of her hair stopped, she reached up to grab hold of her mother's hand for more. But what she felt ended up being a much smaller hand than she remembered. Before she could say anything, she heard her mother's voice, "Now the angels will protect you tonight, mommy."

Mommy? What did her mother mean by mommy? Quickly she opened her eyes. Slightly disoriented, she found herself looking down instead of up. It took her a few more moments before she realized she was mommy. Once she remembered who she was and what she was doing she leaned down just a little further and gave her daughter a tight squeeze then one last kiss, good night. As she got up from the bed, she couldn't help but wondered if her mother had ever experienced what she had just gone through when she gave her the butterfly kisses.

After turning her daughter's bedroom light off Cassandra turned and took one last look in at her daughter. She looked so innocent and peaceful with her eyes closed. Now if only she could be that way when she was awake? With a quiet sigh she walked down the hall only to stop momentarily in front of her son's room to peer inside. She stood just to the corner of the door in order to not be seen as she listened in on her son wrapping up his prayers.

"...and Lord please let Santa bring my parents a nice gift this Christmas for they have been extremely good this year. Amen."

Cassandra felt the warmth of her heart rise to her face and the strange experience she had just encountered seemed to disappear. With renewed joy she made her way into the living room where she noticed it was now well after 10'o clock.

It's Cold Outside

As Cassandra came out from the hallway, she could hear the sounds of dishes clanking against the metal sink while the water continuously ran. Acknowledging her husband was helping her by washing their children's dishes from earlier she entered the living room. Even though she was thankful for his help she still had to wait for him to join her so they could begin the wrapping of presents. To make use of her time she made her way over to the coffee table and leaned over to pick up the remote. After turning it around in the right direction she aimed it at the television then pressed the off button. With the television now off and no other sounds coming from the house she decided to put on some Christmas music. So, she gently placed the remote back down onto the coffee table and made her way toward the entertainment center located in the corner of the room just right of the sofa.

On the top shelf of the music rack just next to the entertainment center she placed her finger on the first CD to her left and read the title to herself. Then slowly she moved her finger to the next and did the same. She continued across the spine of each case until she finally spotted the one CD she knew had their favorite romantic Christmas song. It was Mercer's interpretation of a Frank Loesser song sung by Bing Crosby and Doris Day.

With the one she wanted in front of her, she took her finger and placed it in the top corner of the case. Then with a little force she pulled it out from its snug spot. Once it was in her hand, she carried it over to the stereo that lay waiting on top of the entertainment center to be turned on. After pressing the power button, she lowered her hand and pushed the button labeled CD. When the screen acknowledged her request, she pressed the button to raise the door. As it slowly opened, she pried the case apart then pressed the center in order to pop the CD out. With her forefinger and thumb, she carefully grabbed hold the disc then gently lifted it up and placed it inside the CD player.

As the CD spun around waiting to be acknowledged she turned the case over and looked for the track number of their favorite song. Once she found the track number, she repeated it in her head as she began pressing the forward button until it lit up with the number she wanted. Then just as the song began to play, she felt two arms lightly wrapped around her waist. She knew in an instance who it was and after turning around she playfully pushed her husband away as she began to sing, "I really can't stay."

"But baby it's cold outside." Sean pulled his wife in closer to him.

Cassandra pushed away again this time he caught her by the hand. "I've got to go away."

At the same time Sean spun his wife back into his arms. "But baby, it's cold outside."

"This evening has been..."

"Been hoping' that you'd drop in."

"So very nice." At that moment, her husband let go and grabbed hold of her hands.

The two continued battling verses back and forth as they acted out each line. But when the song had a brief musical interruption Cassandra took advantage of the moment. She took her hands from around his waist and moved them in between their bodies. Then with her open palms against his chest she raised them up until they fell upon his shoulders. When she heard a slight moan escape his lips, she wrapped her hands behind his neck and without warning used them to pull his head in closer to hers.

As their lips met the romance of the season took over. The longer they kissed the more their passion grew. Soon the song that started it all drifted into the background. Neither one seemed to care they had missed their queue for all that matter now was each other.

Unfortunately, like everything else, all good things had to come to an end at some point. As their lips separated Cassandra laid her head upon her husband's shoulder. The music came back into the forefront, and they continued to sing to each other in a whisper as they swayed back and forth in each other's arms.

At the last musical pause Cassandra lifted her head from her husband's shoulder and looked deeply into his eyes. With their eyes locked they sang out the last verse together, "Oh, but baby it's cold outside."

Still holding onto his wife Sean raised his hand and brushed the hair from her face. He then gently placed it behind her ear as he whispered, "You look even more beautiful tonight."

"Even in my pajamas?" asked Cassandra as she looked up into his smoldering hazel eyes.

"Even in your pajamas."

"In that case..." Cassandra paused as she took a hold of his pajama collar and began rubbing it then continued, "you look very dashing in yours."

Feeling his pulse pounding against places his wife had not touched, but hoped she would he quickly suggested, "Do you want to play the song again?"

Unaware of her husband's turmoil she answered, "No, let's just let the CD play its course. Besides the children should be asleep in a few more minutes and we still need to wrap the gifts."

Somewhat disappointed in her answer he slouched just a little, but it must have been just enough to catch his wife's attention. When she pushed her toes and gave him a kiss on the cheek, he knew she was promising him what he wanted after they were done. "I'll go check on them."

As soon as the last word fell out of his mouth her husband quickly released her. Now she was left standing in the middle of the floor feeling the cold draft he had created behind him. She wrapped her arms around herself to fight off the chill as she watched the cause of her discomfort disappear into the darkened hallway. With nothing else to do she stayed put and waited for his return.

Keeping a close eye on her watch, she noticed time seemed to be ticking slower than earlier. With so much more to do before morning she began to wonder what could be keeping her husband so long. She started to tap her fingers on her arms when he finally reappeared, nodding his head to reassure her, they were indeed asleep.

Now she could sneak into the hall closet where they kept the Christmas wrapping paper, along with the boxes of ribbons and bows, without being seen. Quietly she made her way down the hall towards the closet. When she reached the door, she slowly pulled it open hoping her husband had fixed the squeak as per her request earlier in the day.

"Perfect," she whispered when no sound came from the old hinges. Happy with the results she knelt down and towards the back on the floor she grabbed the first packet of wrapping paper and pulled it out. She then reached back in and pulled out two more packets. With her arms now full she stood up then headed back into the living room. When she reached the middle of the floor, she carefully placed the wrapping paper down before heading back toward the closet to pull out the box she needed.

Standing back in front of the closet she looked up at the very top shelf knowing she would have to get the box down by herself once she found it. She read the white labels she had purposely placed on the side of each box until she found the one labeled ribbons and bows. Luckily for her the box hung slightly past the shelf, so standing on the balls of her feet she reached up and used her fingertips to coax the box out further. When it began to teeter, she grabbed a hold of the sides then pulled the box out the rest of the way. Relieved it didn't fall she cradled it close to her and carried it back to the space where she had left the other stuff.

Back in the living room she placed the box on the floor next to the coffee table. Before she had a chance to open it, she heard the garage door open and glanced up. Her husband came towards her carrying two of the bags filled with the gifts they had bought and stored away for this day. She patiently waited until he was almost in front of her before pointing to the empty spot, she had already picked out for him to place the bags. When he was done and headed back to the garage she proceeded to open the box.

She glanced inside then began to pull out the items in order of their use. First came out the spools of ribbon, then bags of bows, followed by the sheets of sticker labels. Liking things organized she sat down and moved everything around in their correct order according to her. She then took one last look at her set up. Something didn't seem right. She mentally walked back through everything when she noticed they still needed scissors, tape and a couple of pens. Not wanting her husband to know she, of all people, forgot anything, she quickly jumped up and made her way into the children's playroom.

Sean had returned from the garage with the remaining bags of loot to find his wife wasn't there. So, he assumed the bags went in the same spot and placed them alongside the others. With all the presents now inside, he turned around and upon spotting the gift-wrapping stuff he took it upon himself to make a spot on the floor for him to sit. Not wanting to wait for his wife to return he started to go through the different rolls of wrapping paper hoping to find the right one to wrap the gift he had bought for his wife. He wasn't sure exactly what he was searching for, but one thing he knew was it had to have angels on it. With that in mind he picked up the first package of five and tore it open. One by one he pulled out each roll and carefully looked it over. When he decided it wouldn't do, he threw it back onto the pile. He continued to tear through the next two packages until he had found a beautiful silver foil like paper with colorful angels and stars printed on it. Not knowing when his wife would return, he quickly hid the perfect paper behind him and began the search for the perfect bow.

Reaching over the messed-up pile of wrapping paper he had created, he grabbed for the bag of unopened bows. Trying to hurry he ripped it open sending the contents inside flying up into the air and landing everywhere.

"Sean!" What, on earth are you doing?" Cassandra quietly yelled as she entered the room. She was furious with the mess her husband had managed to create in such a short period of time.

"Shhh...I thought I would just help by opening a few things." As his wife stepped closer Sean leaned back trying to hide the wrapping paper he took. When she stopped, she was standing over him with pens and tape in one hand while the other was clinching tightly onto a pair of scissors.

After awhile she noticed her husband had been staring at her hand. When she looked down, she realized she had been gripping onto the scissors with the pointed ends downward as if she was going to stab him. She knew she wasn't that mad, so to make him feel more at ease she relaxed her grip and handed them over to him, but not without saying, "I appreciate the thought, Hun, but I had everything organized."

Understanding now he had hurt his wife's feelings he apologized. He waited until his wife had retreated to the empty spot, she had made for herself earlier before sitting back up. Then to move things along he asked, "So...who is wrapping whose gifts this year?"

After getting herself comfortable and making sure she had enough room to do her work she handed her husband a pen and a roll of tape. As she snuggled back into her spot she stated, "You get Ronnie this year."

"Ok. Then I'll start separating the gifts." As Sean reached behind him to grab the first bag. He then snuck the wrapping paper he had hidden and placed it underneath the other bags for later. Hopefully, she wouldn't notice it was missing as they wrapped the other gifts. When it was completely out of view, he brought the bag he had a hold of to his side. After untying the knot, he opened the bag then one by one he took the gifts out. The ones that belonged to his son he set aside while the ones for his daughter he gladly handed over to his wife.

When all four of the bags were empty the two sat concentrating on measuring, cutting, taping and decorating each gift, only pausing to change the music when the CD had completed its cycle. As time went on the pile of unwrapped gifts grew smaller as the gift-wrapped presents grew larger. Then before they knew it a couple of hours had passed and finally there were no more unwrapped gifts.

As Cassandra placed the final touch on her last present she said, "There...We can now put them under the tree."

She then took the present and placed it along with the pile behind her. However, when she turned back around, she noticed her husband was gone. As she began looking around the living room she wondered when he had left and where he had gone off to. Then, as if out of nowhere, her husband had reappeared, stoking the fire.

"I'll be there in just a minute," answered Sean as he smiled to his wife, all the while thinking to himself how close he had cut it. He knew his wife was a perfectionist when it came to gift wrapping and she had always taken her time to get each seam and fold just right. This little quirk of hers gave him the advantage to sneak off and wrap his gift to her.

As she waited for her husband to finish stoking the fire she began to clean up the gift-wrapping mess. She placed all the unused ribbons, bows and labels back into the box for next year and closed the lid. Then before taking the box back to the closet, she made sure she had the remaining wrapping paper together. Knowing they couldn't go back in their original packages she went into the garage to find a large plastic garbage bag to store them in. When she found one located on top of the water heater, she grabbed it and headed back inside. The winter cold made her shiver as she entered the house, but she wasn't going to let it get the best of her. Her goal now was to clean up before moving on to the next thing on her list.

When everything was finally back in place she stood beside her husband in front of the Christmas tree. A small smirk crossed her lips for she enjoyed being the one in charge of placing the presents under the tree. She had already visualized exactly where each present would be placed in order by size, color and name. Now all she had to do was point to the present she wanted her husband to hand to her and put it where it belonged. She started with the largest gifts first for they belonged towards the back of the tree. As the sizes and the piles were getting smaller, she was running out of room, so with the smallest ones she decided to place them on the branches of the tree.

The task ended up taking longer than she had scheduled, but once it was completed, she was thrilled with the results. Now it was time to move on to her duty of filling the stockings while her husband had the duties of eating the cookies, drinking the milk and answering the letter he had written to Santa from his children.

Sean had just closed the fireplace screen and got up to walk over to his recliner when his wife came up beside him ready to fill the stockings. He gave her a quick peck on the cheek then hurried out of her way. When he reached his chair, he made himself comfortable. He then reached over to the TV tray and grabbed one of the cookies from the plate. As he brought the snicker doodle to his lips with one hand the other grabbed a piece of blank paper and began to answer the letter to Santa. Luckily, the questions he wrote only needed short answers as planned. But when it came time to draw the picture of Rudolph, he knew it would be a challenge.

After taking the last bite of his cookie he reached over for the glass of milk to wash it down. As he took a drink his eyes stared down at the enormous space of white. He then lowered his glass hoping the paper would give him a clue on what to draw. When an idea popped into his head, he returned the glass of milk to the tray and began to draw.

The horns were the easiest so that was where he started. He then made his way to the head trying to sketch a side view of Rudolph. When the head was completed, he added the eye, mouth and red nose before stopping briefly to take in his progress. Pleased with himself he grinned. Then after picking up another cookie and placing it into his mouth he started to draw the neck. The flow of the pencil etched lightly upon the paper as he had made a long line from under the head to where he thought the body should begin. 'So far so good,' he thought to himself as he lifted up the pencil and carefully placed it back down on the paper at the top of the head where he drew the upper part of the neck.

Everything was going along smoothly for Cassandra as she hummed along with the Christmas tune that was playing. It seemed all was well with her husband until she was in the middle of filling the stocking that belonged to their daughter when she heard a loud huff followed by the crinkling sound of paper. She immediately stopped what she was doing and turned towards her husband. "What's the matter Honey?"

Surprised by his wife's question Sean lowered the glass of milk he had just placed into his mouth and answered, "It's this darn reindeer. I can draw the head alright, but when it comes to the neck and body, I end up with something even I can't recognize."

"Well then why don't you just draw the head?"

"I can't." Sean picked up another piece of blank paper and started over again.

"Why not," Cassandra quietly asked as she went about filling her daughter's stocking.

"If you remember honey, I did that last year." Once again Sean crumbled up the piece of paper he had been working on and threw it on the floor.

Cassandra slid in the candy cane as the final touch in the stocking before walking over to her husband to offer him some encouragement. As she knelt down beside him, she stretched her arm out and with her hand she took the angel cookie from the plate. Then while taking a bite, she handed her husband another blank piece of paper. She raised the hand that held the cookie and put it in front of her mouth, "Maybe you should draw Rudolph's other end. I'm sure you can do that."

Please with his wife's suggestion he allowed himself to grin slightly. He began to draw the outline of the backend and within minutes he had his picture for his children completed. Feeling better he reached over one last time and grabbed a cookie while his wife took the paper from his lap.

"It looks wonderful. See I knew you could do it." Cassandra rose up onto her knees and gave her husband a kiss on the cheek.

"I couldn't have done it without you by my side Mrs. Claus."

"Why thank you Mr. Claus," Cassandra said before taking the last bite of her cookie.

Plopping his hands onto the arm rest Sean closed his eyes while his mouth opened wide and yawned. When he opened his eyes, he looked at his wife and said, "Well, I guess my work here is done."

"Not quite Santa."

His wife held a cookie and a half glass of milk up in his face. Sean placed one hand on his belly and complained, "I'm full. I can't eat another bite."

Knowing how to pull on her husband's sympathy Cassandra pushed out her bottom lip and fluttered her eyelashes at him. Within seconds she heard the sweet surrender as her husband mumbled something under his breath while taking the cookie and glass from her hands. "That's a good Santa. You really didn't want to disappoint one of your children by leaving a cookie behind?"

As he crammed the last of the frosted treat into his mouth Sean realized something, "Hey now! You could have eaten that cookie."

Cassandra laughed as she stood up, "I could have. But they were left for Santa. Besides I had already eaten the one left for me."

Now with his belly full and his work done, Sean made his way out of the recliner and began to head towards their bedroom. But before reaching the hallway he paused and turned, "Are you coming?"

"Not right at this minute. I still have a few things to do before the kids get up in another six to seven hours." Cassandra gracefully made her way into her husband's arms and gave him one last kiss before letting him go off to bed.

With the house all to herself Cassandra went into the kitchen and grabbed her empty cup from earlier. She rinsed it out then filled it back up with water before placing it in the microwave. As she waited for the water to boil, she went out into the living room and wrapped her husband's gift. She then walked over to the fireplace and filled her husband's stocking. When the microwave beeped, she went back into the kitchen and opened the door. Carefully she pulled out the cup by the handle so not to burn herself and placed it on the countertop. With the water still bubbling in the cup she opened the package she held in her hand and dumped the mixture into the hot water. Then with a spoon she stirred it until it had all dissolved. With the cup full she cautiously made her way to the sofa where she had planned to spend the next half hour or so.

After putting down her drink on the coffee table she grabbed one of the throw pillows from the sofa and propped it against the arm. But before getting comfortable she retrieved the TV guide and a pen. Then stretching out on the sofa she pulled up down the quilt and covered herself up. Now she was ready to begin the last of her tasks. As she flipped through the pages dated for December 25th, she took her time as she read each program offered by time and channel. When she found a Christmas special, she thought her children would enjoy, she took her pen and marked a star beside it.

However, sometimes she would find more than one special scheduled at the same time, so she would mark them all but made an extra star next to the one she liked best. As time wore on, she became sleepy. Part of it was due to the warmth of the chocolate and the other from the continuous reading. Barely able to keep her eyes open, she lowered the guide onto her lap and glanced down at her watch. It was now a quarter after two in the morning. 'Maybe I'll just rest my eyes for a moment,' she thought to herself. She then pulled back on the curtains and took one more glance at the snow that was now only lightly coming down. After releasing the curtain, she slid under the quilt and closed her eyes. As she dosed off into a light slumber, she thought she heard a faint female voice calling her name from a distance.

"Cassandra..."

Presents

"Cassandra..." The voice called out again from the darkness. Cassandra was too tired to try and figure out who kept calling her name, so she just rolled over hoping it would go away. Unfortunately, whoever it was seemed very persistent for once again she heard her name, only this time the voice sounded closer and deeper. It was deep enough to make her body shake.

"Cassandra, wake up."

"Please don't make me. I have no pain here," she quietly mumbled. Then slowly the sensations came back, and she could feel someone's hand shaking her arm. Soon afterwards her ears were able to tune into the noise in the background. When she realized the sounds were coming from her children she awakened and rolled over. She could now see her husband leaning over her and understood it had been him calling, which meant she had overslept, and it was now Christmas morning. Somewhat embarrassed by letting time slip by her she asked, "What time is it?"

Passing off her other remark as a bad dream, Sean knelt down on the floor beside her. He then glanced over at the clock upon the mantle and answered, "It's a little past six."

"Oh honey. I'm so sorry," Cassandra apologized as she pushed herself up against the arm of the sofa. "I didn't mean to nap so long."

Sean chuckled a little for he understood his wife's need to have everything perfect. His only regret was it kept her from keeping the promise she had made to him the night before. So, to remind her he reached up with his hand and gently placed it on the side of her face, allowing her to rest her head upon it. He then whispered, "I forgive you," before moving his lips towards hers'. As their lips lightly touched their breathing became erratic. But before they could go any further, they were interrupted by the screams of excitement.

"Mommy's awake! Mommy's awake!" yelled Ronnie and Elicia. They had been peeking around the corner from the hallway waiting and watching their parents. So, it was no coincidence they yelled out when they did. They had important things to accomplish today and were not going to let their parents prolong them. When they finally got the okay from their father they came out from their hiding place and rushed towards them.

When he reached the end of the sofa where his mother was Ronnie began to jump up and down. Then with a big cheesy grin he asked, "Can we look in our stockings now?"

"Yeah, Can we?" Elicia just stood in front of the coffee table with her hands locked together with her head tilted slightly to the right and her bottom lip puckered out.

"I wonder you she got that from?" Sean sarcastically asked before getting up and leaving his wife's side. As he walked over towards the fireplace, he could hear the excitement in the giggles that seemed to stay close behind him. Once he reached the fireplace he turned, then one by one he picked up his children up so they could take their own stockings off the hooks. After lowering the last child back to the floor, he leaned over to remind them, "Now you know the rules. You have to wait until everyone has theirs before you can open them."

A slight ah escaped Ronnie and Elicia's lips as they hugged their stockings close to their chests. In order to comply they waited impatiently, watching as their father take his time taking down the last two remaining stockings. As soon as he had the loot in his hands they turned around and waited for him to pass. Then keeping one foot behind they followed like little lambs until they reached the sofa where their mother had made room for everyone.

"Ok. Does everyone have a spot?" Cassandra asked as she leaned a little closer to the coffee table. When her husband reached across their two children and handed her her stocking she gave the orders, "Dump!"

All at once the loud crashing sound of objects hitting the wooden table echoed through the otherwise quiet house. But even though Cassandra had dumped hers along with the family she decided to sit back a little bit. As she watched her children's movements it did not surprise her when she saw them separate the food from the toys. Yet it did take her aback when she noticed her son had not only separated the food but had his fruit in a different pile from the nuts and the nuts by their kind. On the other hand, her daughter was typical for she only had the two piles. Then somehow her daughter managed to un-wrap the candy cane and had it hanging from her mouth as she tore into the first small, wrapped toy.

Contentment filled her heart to see how excited her children were with the small trinkets they found in their stockings. As she leaned farther back a cold sensation brushed across the back of her neck. She turned her head towards the window and looked through the small opening of the curtains, then gasped.

"What is it?" Sean asked as he pulled out the wrapped present his wife had snuck into his stocking. By the look on her face, he knew he needed to see for himself to understand. So, he put down the gift and turned away from the festivities to pull back the curtains. To his amazement the snow had stopped, but not before leaving behind enough snow to be even with the windowsill.

"I guess this means our families won't be able to make it over for Christmas dinner," stated Cassandra with sadness in her voice. As she lowered her head in disappointment she began to twist her fingers together in her lap. All her hard work planning and preparing for her year to host the Christmas dinner just went out the window. Her heart sank more as she thought about her family and how she had been looking forward to seeing them and impressing them with her new culinary skills. She was now left to wonder what she was going to do with all the food she had bought. Some of it she knew would keep if frozen. But there was the case of the pies she had baked the night before. To be exact there were two pumpkin, one Dutch apple and one black berry sitting on the counter. If the snow did not melt away soon, they would have to be thrown out.

Seeing how upset his wife was Sean let go of the curtains. There had to be something he could do to make it right for her. But until he could figure out what that was, he said, "We'll figure out something. But for now, let's continue with our Christmas morning."

Cassandra raised her head and looked into her husband's eyes. There in the deep blue pools she could see a slight twinkle letting her know everything was going to be all right. And with that reassurance she smiles.

"Oh cool!" Ronnie's eyes grew wider as he stared out the window with his sister by his side. "Can we go out and play?"

Sean chuckled at their enthusiasm then offered, "I'll tell you what. You can go outside and play, or...," he was briefly interrupted when his children started jumping up and down cheering, "...or we can open presents."

"Presents! Presents!"

"Ok, presents it is. Now stop jumping on the furniture before your mother gets mad and put away your stockings."

As her children plopped their bottoms back down on the sofa Cassandra went to the kitchen to make them some coffee and hot chocolate. She grabbed the coffee pot from the maker and held it under the faucet. When the pot was a quarter of the way full, she swished the water around then poured it out. She repeated the action only one more time before allowing the water to finally fill the pot. When it was full she stood over the coffee maker and poured in the water. From there she replaced the pot back into its spot then turned it on. As the coffee maker gurgled and steamed, she reached into the cabinet above and grabbed out four mugs. Two of the mugs she sat next to the coffee maker while the other two she held under the faucet in order to fill them partially full. When the water was at the right height, she turned off the faucet then carried the mugs to the microwave.

After closing the door and setting the timer she leaned against the counter and watched the mugs spin around. The next thing she knew she heard her name being called again.

"Cassandra..."

This time she thought she recognized the voice. But it wasn't until she heard it say, "...Merry Christmas..." that she knew and without thinking she whispered to herself, "Mom."

At that moment, the beeping of the microwave snapped her out of her trance. After blinking her eyes Cassandra could not help but wonder what it meant as she took out the mugs from the microwave and placed them next to the others. Automatically she reached over to the corner behind the coffee maker where she kept the box of hot coco and grabbed out two envelopes. Pinching the tops between her fingers she shook the envelopes three times before tearing them open. Then one by one she dumped the mixture into the mugs. After stirring them with the spoon she had sitting next to the coffee maker she set them aside then turned her attention towards the coffee.

The first cup was the easiest to fix because her husband drank his black. However, her coffee needed a little more doctoring, so she spooned in three spoons full of sugar and three heaping spoons of nondairy creamer, and that was for a normal day. Yet today was not normal because it was a holiday and since she added a little bit of ground cinnamon to the coffee grounds there was still something missing.

After she placed the mugs on the tray she went over to the refrigerator and grabbed out a can of whipped cream. She shook the can before she pulled off the top, then aiming the nozzle towards the rim of the first mug she pressed it with her thumb. As the whip cream began to squirt out, she used it to seal the rim of the mug. Once that was completed, she continued to move her hand in a spiral motion towards the center and topping it off with a mound in the middle. She repeated the same routine with two more mugs leaving her husband's the only one bare. Now with everything perfect she carried the tray into the living room.

As she entered, she caught her children shaking the presents trying to figure out what was inside. "Ah...hum!" she let out as she gave her children a stern look. She then sat the tray on the coffee table and asked them, "Now where is your father?"

In the garage Sean had been loading his arms up with firewood. After seeing all the snow outside he figured he would need to rebuild the fire and keep it going just in case. When his arms were full, he made his way to the door. As he was about to turn the knob he happened to glance over at the far corner of the garage. Seeing the snowplow he had an idea. With a smirk on his face, he juggled the logs around so he could turn the knob and head inside the house.

"Oh, there you are," said Cassandra when she saw her husband walk in with his arms full. She continued to watch him as he made his way over to the fireplace and dropped the logs beside it. When he proceeded to open the screen, she decided to grab his coffee and carried it over to him. The whole short distance she kept in her mind what had happened in the kitchen. So, by the time she reached her husband she knelt down beside him then quietly said, "I know this might sound strange. But while I was in the kitchen, I thought I heard my mother's voice."

Before saying anything, Sean finished crumpling up the piece of newspaper he had in his hand and stuffed it in between two logs. He then turned towards his wife and took the mug of coffee she had held out to him. After raising the mug up to his nose, he took a deep breath. The slight hint of cinnamon made his mouth water. Eager to take a sip he lowered it to his lips. But before he had the chance to take one, he noticed his wife was waiting for a response, so he said, "Honey, I'm sure you just thought you heard your mother."

Disappointed with his comment Cassandra sat back onto the bottom of her feet as she watched her husband take a sip from his mug. She waited until he swallowed before adding, "I know what I heard Sean. She even wished me a Merry Christmas."

"Well then, that explains it." He put down his mug and crumpled up a few more pieces of newspaper. Then, while stuffing them between logs in different places he continued, "Cassandra you are worried that your mother will not be able to make it due to the snow. So, your subconscious has decided to let you hear her if you aren't able to see her."

"I guess," said Cassandra. She looked down at her husband's coffee mug hoping her husband was right. Then realizing it was the only explanation that made sense she looked back up. "I'll give her a call after we un-wrap the gifts."

"That sounds like a wonderful idea. Now go take care of the kids while I get this fire going again." Sean finished placing the splinter logs on top of the newspapers then stood up. He then held out his hand and helped his wife up before retrieving the box of matches from the mantle.

When Cassandra turned around, she noticed the children were quietly shaking the presents under the tree in hopes not to be heard. She decided to teach them a lesson and tiptoed softly up behind them. When she got close enough behind them, she asked, "What did I tell you earlier?"

Hearing her mother's voice so close Elicia jumped making her drop the present she had in her hand. As she turned around to face her, she crinkled up her nose letting her mother know she disapproved of her tactics. If that wasn't enough, she said, "Mom, you scared us half to death."

"Well, if you had done like you were told I wouldn't have scared you," stated Cassandra. After making her children place the presents back in place she turned them around and directed them towards the coffee table. After having them sit on the floor, she handed them their hot chocolate then picked up the TV Guide and remote. She glanced down at her watch then flipped to the pages back and found the first special she had marked. When she turned the television to the station, she heard her son say,

"Perfect timing mom, Rudolph the Red Nose Reindeer just started."

Happy to have her children finally entertained, Cassandra glanced over her shoulder in time to see her husband closing the screen and collecting his coffee. On that note she put down the objects in her hand and picked up her mug carefully. When she held it close to her mouth, she quickly tried to lick off the whip cream that had begun to melt and was now running down the side. After gaining control she was just about to take a sip when her husband came up from behind her and wrapped his arms around her waist. He then whispered in her ear.

"Are you ready?"

With her hands cupped around her mug and her eyes closed Cassandra replied, "Um...yes," then her eyes sprung open. "Oh! You meant the presents."

"Yes, I meant the presents." Sean chuckled as he snuggled a little closer. "Why? What else did you have in mind?"

"Get a room you two," Elicia inserted without taking her eyes off the television.

Shocked by her six- year- olds' remark, Cassandra quickly took a sip from her mug as her husband let go and made his way to the tree. This year she had clean up duty while her husband got to hand out the presents. With their rolls reversed, she found a nice spot next to her children on the floor and armed herself with the big plastic bag she had hidden under the table.

Soon the joy of Christmas took over as the special had been forgotten and the first gift held up. The gift was small in comparison to the rest, but it still had been wrapped with care. The white paper held green printed trees upon it and a single bow that matched. The label bared a silver border that encircled a small, decorated Christmas tree on the left side leaving space for the recipient and the giver's name. Everyone waited in silence eager to find out who would be the one to receive the beautiful gift. Then at last the name was read and the tree covered gift was handed to its owner.

Cassandra watched as her son tore into the paper that contained what now belonged to him. And when his face lit up with joy after seeing his new I-Pod she knew they had made the right choice. Since her son had been first, she knew her daughter was next. She leaned back against the coffee table as her husband held up the next gift wrapped in holly leaves and berries with a red bow on top. The gift was similar in size and shape as the previous, but the only difference was how her daughter un-wrapped it. She started by carefully prying off the bow from the paper then methodically peeling the tape back. If the tape began to tear the paper, she would lay it back in place and find another spot. Finally, when all the tape had been removed, she slowly unfolded each side. Now all that was left to do was unroll it.

During this time Cassandra had glanced around at the others and could feel they were growing impatient. Yet, she let the feeling pass for she understood how important it was for her daughter to save the precious Christmas paper from her first gift as a keepsake. Then a screech of glee escaped her daughter, and she held up her very first music player of her own. Relieved it was finally over she relaxed. Now it was her turn.

Since neither she nor her husband had a small gift under the tree she remembered the ones from their stockings. She didn't remember opening hers and hoped her husband hadn't opened his either. Holding onto that hope she turned and to her surprise she found them still lying on the coffee table, unopened, and collected them. After turning back around she propped up on her knees then reached over and handed her husband his gift.

As per their tradition she always got to open her gift first. With a smile on her face, she sat back down on her feet then ran her fingers over the silver bow that was as big as the gift itself. Seeing the special wrapping paper her husband used she almost started to cry. Then when she glanced over at him, she realized everyone was waiting for her. So, trying not to destroy the wrapping she carefully pried the bow's tape from the paper but left it attached to the ribbon. She then gently wiggled the ribbon over to the corners until it was loose enough to slide off keeping it in tacked. Fortunately for her the ribbon was the only thing that held the paper in place and the Angel along with the lone star was saved. Now all that was left was to find out what was inside. She grabbed hold of the seam and began to unroll the paper from its contents until she was left with only a white box in her hand. Knowing it was jewelry her heart began to pound as her hands began to shake. After taking a deep breath to steady herself she slowly lifted one side of the lid so she could peer inside.

Upon seeing the sparkling silver piece, she flipped off the lid. When she saw the rest of it, she held her hand over the center of her chest. She was speechless as she lifted out the silver necklace with two silver charms in the shape of footprints dangling from it. As she held it up for everyone to see she noticed each footprint held a birthstone. Taking a closer look, she realized they represented their children's birth months. As tears began to fill her eyes she looked over at her husband and said, "Oh sweetie, I love it."

The small twinkling of Christmas lights reflecting in his wife's teary hazel eyes told Sean the depth of her meaning. Yet there still was left one more first gift, and it belonged to him. And like his son the wrapping did not mean as much as what awaited him inside just waiting to be discovered. So, without hesitation he tore through the gold foil paper to find an old rustic brown leather box. Puzzled by the familiar box he briefly glanced over towards his wife. She only smiled back at him letting him know he had guest right. As he lifted the lid the old hinges creaked. Then just as he suspected he found himself staring down at the golden object. "It's my great grandfather's pocket watch. But how..."

"Your grandmother gave it to me on our last visit before she died, but not without the instructions that I was not to give it to you until Christmas. She said she wanted to see you open it from heaven." Cassandra could see the emotions build up in her husband's eyes. She knew how much his grandmother meant to him and this was indeed the perfect gift.

No more words needed to be said as Sean closed the leather box and placed it by his side. There were still more presents to give out, so he picked out one for each person and handed them to its rightful owners. After the presents were opened with joyous glee, hugs and thank you, Sean reminded his children to pass over their torn-up wrappings to their mother. He wanted to make sure the clean up afterwards would not hinder anything else they had to do before tonight. So once the papers were picked up and, in the bag, he handed out the next.

Breakfast

After stuffing the last of the wrapping paper into the garbage bag, Cassandra looked up. She wasn't too surprised to see the sight that had unfolded around her. Her children had managed to open every box. And along with their new toys they were sprawled all across the floor, at least the ones that did not need assembling. Not surprisingly, in the very center of it all sat her husband. She couldn't help but giggle as she watched his child like behavior while he played along side their children. At least her husband was occupying their children's time. She turned her attention back towards squashing down the paper then tying the full bag closed. After the knot was completed, she stood up and grabbed hold of the plastic tie strings. But Before taking it out to the garage she leaned the bag against the coffee table so she could change the channel.

As she glanced down at the open page of the TV guide, she noticed the shows she had marked for that morning were almost over. However, she knew deep down her children would be too preoccupied exploring their new treasures to even care. Taking that into consideration she clicked over to another station. It was the last ten minutes of "Frosty's Return", but she knew when it was over the Christmas parade would start. She replaced the remote and the guide back onto the coffee table then lifted the garbage bag off the floor. After putting the loops around one of her wrists she took her other hand and placed it on the bottom to help distribute the weight.

She carried the bag through the path of empty boxes and toys while the rest of her family continued to enjoy their Christmas morning. The sounds of joyous playing left her with a feeling of content as she reached the door to the garage. But when she opened it a rush of bitter coldness hit her face reminding her of what lay outside. Not wanting to endure the cold garage she decided not to turn on the light or go down the steps. She deposits the bag to the side for she knew her husband would take it out to the trash can later. Now it was time to prepare breakfast, so she closed the door leaving the chilled air behind. As she passed through the dining room, she glanced over at her family to see how they were doing. All seemed to be going well, so she entered the kitchen. When she reached the sink, she turned on the faucet to wash off her hands before donning her apron.

Every Christmas morning Cassandra had made her famous seasonal spiced German pancakes, but this year she had something extra to prepare that would assess her skill in time management. She began by making her way to the pantry and collected the bag of flour then sat it on the island counter. Next, she went to the refrigerator and took out the carton of eggs and milk then placed them on the counter alongside the flour. Now the only ingredients she had left to collect were the spices. All her spices were kept in one spot, the cabinet on the wall to the left of the stove. In there on the bottom shelf she found the container of ground cinnamon, cloves, nutmeg, vanilla and salt. After collecting them all she went back to the counter and set them beside the other ingredients. As she looked down at the counter, she knew of only two things left to get, the big glass mixing bowl and the wire whisk.

After she set the last two things on the counter she went over to the stove and turned the oven on to 400 degrees. As the oven preheated, she pulled both of her cast iron skillets from the back burners and scooped in two tablespoons of margarine in each. She then slid the skillets in the oven to heat. Since it would take a couple of minutes for the butter to melt, she turned back to adding the ingredients into the bowl. For her family of four she would have to make a double batch. From memory she dumped in 1 cup of flour, 1 cup of milk, 6 eggs and a dash of salt. As she mixed them with a wire whisk, she continued to add in a few dashes of ground cinnamon, ground cloves, nutmeg and a little vanilla for flavor. When everything was well mixed, she carried the bowl over to the counter by the stove and sat it down. She then opened the drawer next to her and slipped on her oven mitts. Ready for the heat she opened the oven door and pulled out the now hot skillets one by one and sat them on top of the stove to be filled with half of the batter.

When the last drop of batter dripped from the bowl, she tilted it back up and scraped the side with the whisk. Knowing she would only have twenty-five minutes, once she placed the skillets back into the oven, she sat the bowl in the sink then put the oven mitts back on. Carefully she slid the two cast iron skillets back onto the oven rack, closed the door and set the timer. Now the challenge had begun. Quickly she grabbed the eggs and milk from the island counter and placed them back into the refrigerator then pulled out the turkey.

As she carried the thawed-out turkey over to the sink she remembered she needed to call her mother. Too many things to do and not enough time to do it in, but this call was very important, so she had to make it work. After placing the turkey in the empty side of the sink she grabbed the cordless phone from the counter beside her and dialed her mother's number. As the phone rang, she tucked it between her shoulder and chin, freeing her hands to grab a pair of scissors from the knife holder. She then began to cut the plastic bag from the turkey.

She took hold of the legs and carefully snipped under the metal clamp. After making one slit down the length of the legs she realized the phone had rung at least five or six times. She pulled back the scissors and placed them down on the counter. Still holding onto the slit in the bag with one hand she moved her free one up to grab the phone. But before she had the phone from her ear the bag ripped. The turkey twisted out of her hand and dropped into the sink causing the juice to splash up and outward. As she cursed under her breath, she managed to hang up the phone and placed it on the counter next to her. She then hurriedly grabbed a clean towel to wipe off her face.

Hearing the loud thump Sean excused himself from playing dolls with his daughter. As he entered the kitchen, he saw his wife trying desperately to clean off her apron with a towel and asked, "Are you okay?"

"Yeah, I'm fine," Cassandra answered as she turned on the faucet and started to wash off her arms. "It's just the bag ripped, and the turkey slipped out of my hands."

"Would you like some help?" Sean asked as he came up behind her.

After turning off the faucet and grabbing a clean towel from the drawer she turned to her husband. Then as she wiped off her hands and arms she answered, "No, really I'm fine. Go back and have the kids start putting away their new toys. Breakfast should be done in about eighteen minutes."

Sensing something else was bothering her Sean gently grabbed a hold of his wife's arms and looked her straight in the eyes. "If you need me for anything just let me know."

"I will, I promise." Cassandra tried hard not to let her husband know how upset she was. It seemed to work for her husband released her and went back into the living room. Alone once again she took a deep breath. As she let it out a shiver ran up her spine. All of a sudden, she felt a dire need to call her brother. Unfortunately, she was running out of time to get the turkey ready before breakfast was done.

She hurried over to the pantry and collected the roasting pan off the floor. After carrying it over and placing it on the stovetop she went back to the sink. She quickly peeled off the remaining plastic that covered the turkey then pulled out the giblets and the neck from the cavities. After putting them aside she turned on the faucet to rinse off any lingering blood from the turkey before placing it into the roasting pan.

Once the turkey was set in nicely, she went back to the pantry and grabbed the stuffing mix. As time clicked by, she snagged another big glass bowl from the cabinet and placed it on the counter next to the stove. Then without skipping a beat she opened the box of preseason stuffing mix and dumped it into the bowl. She proceeded to mix in the butter and a few other ingredients to add a little more flavor and substance to the stuffing. With the mixture now complete, she took her hand and scooped out some of the stuffing. However, before she was able to stuff the bird the timer on the stove went off, so she dropped the stuffing back into the bowl. She then hurriedly brushed the crumbs off her hands before wiping them on the towel.

After slipping her hands back into the oven mitts she opened the oven door, and the smell of cinnamon and cloves engulfed the room. She carefully grabbed hold of the first cast iron skillet and placed it on top of the stove behind the roasting pan then reached back in to grab the other. While the pancakes were cooling, she turned the temperature down on the oven and went back to stuffing the bird.

She crammed as much stuffing as she could into the cavity between the legs before rebinding them. With more left in the bowl, she pulled the skin down from the neck cavity and stuffed the rest. When there was no stuffing left, she pulled the extra skin over and pinned it in place so none of the stuffing could escape. Next, she poured in two cups of water from the tap. Then before placing the lid on the roaster, she reached up and grabbed a few more seasonings from the cabinet to help enhance the flavor.

"There," she said as she placed the lid on. She opened the oven door and with her mitts on she lowered the top rack then gently slid the pan in the oven. With everything in place, she went to the sink to retrieve the bag for the cooking instructions. Six and a half hours it read, but that was the entire time. She knew she needed to allow at least one hour, with the top off, in order to brown and crisp the skin. So, she readjusted the timer to read five and a half as a reminder to take the lid off. Now she could finish cleaning up and begin preparing the family breakfast.

With an oven mitt on one hand and a spatula in the other she grabbed hold of the handle and scraped around the edges of the skillet to loosen the pancake. Once it was freed, she carried the pan over to the plates she had on the counter behind her. She then carefully lifted the puffed-up pancake out of the pan and slid it onto one of the plates then placed the skillet into the sink. Next, she took out a butter knife from the drawer to cut the German pancake in half for a whole one would be too big for one person to eat. After she made two halves, she scooped one of them up and placed it on another plate only to repeat her actions until there were four. "Ok everybody come tell me what you want on your pancake."

Hearing the word pancake echo down the hallway, Ronnie and Elicia found themselves racing to see who would be the first one to get their food. But their efforts were all for not. As they entered the kitchen, they were disappointed to see their father already waiting to be served. Yet, not wanting to be defeated by his father Ronnie leaned over and whispered into his sister's ear with a plan.

"Ok...ok," Elicia whispered back.

With his sister backing him up Ronnie approached their father from behind. When he got close enough, he tugged on the back of his pajama shirt. He waited until his father acknowledged him then made his proposal, "Dad, I know you won, and you have the right to be first. But I was thinking...being the honorable gentleman that you are... maybe you could allow ladies first then youngest to oldest."

Sean was about to clamp his fingers onto the plate being handed to him when his wife snatched it back. "Hey!"

"Well, your son makes a very good argument," stated Cassandra as she held the plate close to her.

"Oh, he's good," Sean whispered under his breath. He still wanted to be first, but after looking at his wife he knew she was waiting for an answer, and it had better be the one she was expecting. Finally, he reluctantly bowed before his daughter and said, "You first my lady."

Elicia stepped forward with a little smile upon her face. She was glad that her brother's plan had worked, and he was nice enough to make it work out that she got to go first. She listened as her mother called out all the choices to top off her pancake. When her mother was done, she found herself struggling between the strawberry syrup and the powder sugar. She then remembered it already had cinnamon, ground cloves, nutmeg and a hint of vanilla. Thinking about the delicious spices that made it smell so good, she finally figured out what she wanted, "Powder sugar please."

After her mother lightly covered her pancake in white, she took her plate and fork. Then before taking her place at the dining table, she turned to her brother and silently thanked him.

With one plate out of the way Cassandra slid the next one over. When she turned back to her remaining family, she noticed her husband had his hands out waiting for her to hand it over. "Sean, aren't you forgetting something?"

"Oh sorry, I want regular syrup on mine," Sean answered with a grin big enough to show all his teeth.

Placing one hand on her hip and leaning on the other against the counter, Cassandra disappointedly stated, "Ah...No!"

With his grin still frozen in place Sean threw out the one word he thought his wife was waiting for, "Please."

"No Sean. You promised your son youngest to oldest. That means Ronnie is next." She motioned for her son to step forward and claim his breakfast.

"That's not fair!" Sean yelled out as he watched his son smile deviously up at him when he walked by. "I was tricked!"

"Tricked or not you agreed to be served last. And that includes after me." Cassandra winked at her son as she waited for him to choose his topping. Then after pouring the syrup on two of the pancakes, she gave her son his plate and scooted him off. She then took the other into her hand and held it out. By now her husband stood in front of her wearing a frown, so she tapped on his upper arm and tried to get him to take the plate.

Still pouting over his loss Sean looked down at the plate then questioned his wife, "What's this?"

"It's your breakfast silly," answered Cassandra. She then forced the plate into his hand and added, "Now go sit with your children and eat."

"What about you?"

"I'll join you in a minute. I just want to give my brother a quick call." As she let go of the plate she leaned in a little closer and gave her husband a kiss on the lips then sent him away.

Alone in the kitchen once more she picked up the phone and dialed her brother's number. As it rang, she found herself whispering, 'Please pick up Steve, please pick up.' Unfortunately, all she got was his answering machine...

"Beep...Merry Christmas! You have reached the Blanchers.... we'll get back to you... the hospital...thank you...beep."

Only hearing parts of the message Cassandra quickly hung up and frantically dialed her sister's number. "Come on Vicky answer your phone," she quietly said to herself. As the phone continued to ring, she realized there was no answering machine. Again, she hung up. Now how was she supposed to find out what was going on? She found herself left with more questions than answers. As panic began to set in, she glanced over at her family still enjoying their breakfast. She decided to move into the living room so they couldn't see how upset she was. Still thinking about the puzzling message on her brother's answering machine she decided to try his cell phone. After making her way to her recliner she sat down and dialed. Just as it rang the third time a voice answered...

"Cassandra..."

"Steve, thank god I got a hold of you. Is Vicky all right?"

"Yes."

"Thank God!" Cassandra let out a sigh of relief as she placed her hand over her heart. "What about mom?"

"Yes, she is fine. Matter of fact they are both here. Now how are you feeling?"

"I'm fine now. Can you tell me what happened?"

"What do you mean...what happened?"

"I called your house, and the message said you where at the hospital."

"I think you are still a little confused."

"Confused?" Just then a cold eerie sensation swept over her body.

"Cassandra, we are at the hospital visiting you."

Just then she felt a hand touch the one she had rested on the arm rest. She slowly lowered her gaze but all she could see was the hair standing straight up on her arm. Spooked, she quickly hung up and tossed the phone. It slid across the floor until it stopped underneath the coffee table.

"Honey, are you alright?" Sean knelt down then looked up at his wife. When she didn't answer, or make an effort to look at him, he cupped his hands over hers. "Your hands are freezing."

Feeling the warmth return to her body from the touch of her husband, Cassandra blinked and looked down upon his concerned face. Without warning her horror turned into tears. Was she going mad? Did she really hear her brother correctly? No, she couldn't have for how one person could be in two places at once. As the tears began to stream down her cheek her husband reached up and gently wiped them away. She knew then she had to tell him what happened and hoped and prayed he did not think she was crazy. "Sean I just had the strangest thing happen and I don't know where to start."

Still holding onto his wife's hands he replied, "Why don't you start at the beginning, and I will help you make some sense out of this."

Cassandra lowered her head, and stared into her hands, as she re-played in her mind what had happened. With her thoughts all organized she told her husband everything started with the call to her mother. She continued in detail until she reached the part about her brother's answering machine message.

When his wife paused Sean knew she wanted some reassurance he was listening to her. So, he let go of her hands and made himself comfortable in front of her recliner. As he looked up into her eyes, he hoped he would be able to ease her mind. "Ok, tell me what it said, and I will try to figure out the meaning."

Preparing herself Cassandra leaned her head against the head rest and rolled her eyes upward searching her mind for the memory that held the answering machine message. When it popped into the forefront, she lifted her head and looked down at her husband. She replayed the parts she could remember hoping it would not sound stupid.

Sean listened intently to every word and when she finished, he took his time trying to absorb it all. After closing his eyes, he allowed his brain to ponder on what he heard. The longer he thought about it the more he realized there had to be more to the message. He knew he couldn't ask his wife to try harder to remember without upsetting her more, so he worked with what he had and came up with some good ideas.

He remembered his brother in-law's wife liked to volunteer at the children's ward especially around Christmas time. Maybe that was what he was referring to on the answering machine? Before he had a chance to ask his wife about what he was thinking she had already continued to what happened next.

"Naturally upset I came in here and finally reached my brother on his cell."

"So, was he at the hospital?" asked Sean as he watched the expression on his wife's face slowly change.

"Yes."

"Did you find out why he was there?"

"Yes."

"Was it the children's ward?" When his wife answered no he had to rethink the message. What could be another reason for Steve to mention hospital? As he thought about it, he remembered his sister-in-law might have had a layover and met them there. "Was it your sister?"

"No."

The direction his questions where heading was not good, and he knew if his wife answered yes to his next question, she would be inconsolable. However, there was no other way for him to understand so he had to ask, "Was it your...Mother?"

"No."

Relieved, but confused Sean asked one more question, "Ok, was your sister in-law in an accident?"

"No...I don't know..." Tears took control over her eyes again as fear and frustration built up inside her.

"I thought you said your brother told you what happened."

Cassandra raised her hands and covered her face. Her body began to shake as she forced herself to finally tell her husband what was said. "He said they were there to see me."

Bewildered, Sean rose up on his knees and wrapped his arms around his wife to comfort her. He let her cry on his shoulder while he tried to make some sense of what she thought she heard. Maybe the snowstorm had something to do with her state of mind. He knew how important this dinner was to her and the thought of her family not being able to get through the snow might just as well contribute to her illusions. So, gently he pulled her away from his body and began to wipe away the tears from her face. Then in a loving voice he made a suggestion, "How about I give your brother a call?"

"Ok." Cassandra looked directly into her husband's eyes as she nodded and sniffled.

"Alright then," stated Sean. After standing up he reached over and pulled out a tissue from the box next to her chair. He handed it to his wife then patted her on the side of her leg. Before walking away he added, "I'll do that while you go eat."

The Meaning of Family

By the time Cassandra entered the dining room her breakfast was cold, and her children were done. Instead of sitting down to eat she stacked all the plates on top of each other then placed all the forks on top. She then carefully grabbed the stack and carried them off into the kitchen. When she reached the sink, she placed the plates onto the counter then turned on the water. As the water ran into the sink, she grabbed the sponge next to the faucet and began to wipe off the leftovers from the top plate. Once it was cleared of all food, she sat it in the sink and grabbed another. When all the plates were ready, she opened the dishwasher. After pulling out the bottom rack she carefully placed each plate in its rightful spot before cleaning off the silverware and placing them in their own compartment. With the dishwasher now full she added the detergent and started the cycle.

As the methodic sound filled the kitchen, she went over to the oven to check on the turkey. She opened the oven door and pulled out the rack then lifted the lid to the roasting pan. A burst of steam rose along with the faint scent of herbs. When the steam dissipated, she checked the water level to make sure there was still enough to keep the turkey moist.

Before she was done, she heard her children begging her husband to go outside and play. Sadly, she also heard her husband answer no, at least not until he had been able to shovel the walkway to make it safe. Reminded of the snow once more, she replaced the lid onto the roasting pan and slid the rack back into the oven. She then walked back to the sink and glanced out the window. The feeling of despair rose within as she looked at the height of the snow. As she continued to look out the window she heard the sound of footsteps coming up behind her and knew it was her husband.

"I got a hold of your brother."

She slowly turned away from the window to face her husband, partially afraid to hear what he had found out. Yet, she knew she needed to know so she asked, "And?"

"He said he was sorry he missed your call, but they had gone over to pick up your mother." Sean noticed his wife began to open her mouth to say something, so he placed his finger over her lips. "Let me finish." When she closed her mouth, he lowered his finger then said, "They drove from there to the neighboring children's hospital to drop off gifts."

During this time Cassandra had been irritated her husband had not let her speak, so she had been unconsciously tapping her finger on top of the counter. When she realized what she was doing she stopped then asked, "What about my sister?"

"He said Vicky is on her way over to his house since her connecting flight here had been cancelled."

"I guess that explains most of it, but what about our conversation?"

Stepping in a little closer Sean placed his hand upon her shoulder. "Honey, Steve said he never received a call on his cell."

"I know I called him," Cassandra strongly stated.

Trying not to make the matter worse Sean thought hard for an easy way to ask his wife what he thought happened. Unfortunately, there were none. "Do you think it is possible that you accidentally dialed the wrong number?"

"I guess..." Cassandra began to answer then added, "But I heard Steve's voice."

"Honey," started Sean as he looked into her eyes, "remember you were set on talking with him. Maybe you just thought you were speaking with Steve."

Thinking her husband must really believe she was going crazy she lowered her head. How could she make him understand what she knew she heard? Her feelings changed when she realized he was just trying to help with the touch of his hand under her chin. She allowed him to lovingly lift up her chin until their eyes met. As she gazed into his eyes, she fought back the urge to cry and said, "Maybe you're right. Maybe I allowed myself to hear what I wanted to."

"Sweetheart, I have an idea." Sean lowered his hand and glanced past his wife out the window. "How about I take the snowplow and clear the road. When I'm done, I can go door to door through our neighborhood and invite anyone who had to cancel their Christmas plans to our house for dinner?"

The sad little frown that had sat upon Cassandra's face soon turned into a pleasant smile, for she now truly understood what her mother had told her about family. Family was not just flesh and blood. Families were the people you chose to share with and cared for. And that definition fits their neighborhood community. Filled with a new kind of happiness she lunged forward and wrapped her arms around her husband's neck. "Thank you."

"You're welcome," Sean whispered in her ear. With his wife happy again he backed up a bit from the embrace to get a better look at her. She stared back at him with a smile that lit up the room and he knew he had to make good on his promise. Now faced with a big job he said, "Why don't I go and get dressed while you continue your preparations for dinner."

Cassandra could not find the words to express how happy he had just made her, so with her hands still wrapped around his neck she pulled him closer. The warmth and power of the kiss that soon followed made her raise her hand and run her fingers through his hair. Passion soon took over as his lips parted from hers and claimed her neck. A tingling sensation ran down her body and she was just about to melt into his arms when they were interrupted by their children.

Reluctantly she let go of her husband and leaned against the counter. When she turned her head towards her children, she could tell that they had heard at least part of their conversation by the way they begged and pleaded with their eyes to go outside. She then glanced back over at her husband and asked, "Well?"

Sean found himself once again torn between what he truly wanted and what his wife wanted him to do. Life was so much simpler before having children, but when he looked at his children, he could not refuse those cute little faces.

"Ok," he answered, "but I want you to understand that I am not going outside to play. I have a promise to keep to your mother so it will be all work."

It did not matter to Ronnie what they did as long as he got to be outside in the snow and spend some time with his father. "That's ok dad."

However, Elicia only wanted to go outside to play in the snow and to see how her snowman was doing. "Daddy is it ok if I just go out for a little bit to make angels?"

Cassandra watched as her husband pondered over the question. She knew he was willing to brave the cold and snow to make her happy, but now found himself struggling to find a way to make his daughter happy as well. In order to help him out of his dilemma she knelt down upon one knee and waved her daughter over. When her daughter reached her, she said, "I'll tell you what. I will come out and help you make angels as long as when we are done you will come inside and help me get things ready for dinner."

"Deal," answered Elicia as she wrapped her hands around her mother's neck.

"Then it's settled. You guys go and get changed while I finish up in here before joining you." After Cassandra gently pulled her daughter's arms off of her, she stood up and smiled as her children ran out of the room. It felt good to have her daughter agree to help her prepare this special dinner for their special type of family this holiday season. With the children gone she went back to wiping down the counters as if nothing had happened between her and her husband. Yet, it seemed her husband had other plans. As he came up behind her she didn't bother turning around when she asked, "Sean, shouldn't you be getting dressed if you are going outside?"

Sean stopped dead in his tracks then quietly backed up until his back touched the counter across from his wife. As he stood there, he couldn't help but admire her shapely form as she leaned over the counter. If only they were alone in the house. He would take advantage of the time alone to show his wife a very Merry Christmas. As soon as the thought crossed his mind the sound of something dropping into the sink vanquished it. "Ah...yes. I'm going right now."

After placing the bottle of dish soap back onto the counter Cassandra turned her head just in time to catch a glimpse of the smirk her husband wore on his face as he turned to leave. Her cheeks began to flush for she knew what was on his mind and she too had similar thoughts. Unfortunately, she had a lot of things to do before dinner would be ready, so she had to settle with watching her husband's manly physique walk out of her sight. With a heavy sigh for what was not going to happen she redirected her attention back towards wiping out the dirty sink.

When she finished cleaning up the kitchen, she made her way down the hall stopping briefly to check on her children. She thought since they had not come out, they might need her help. But much to her surprise she found her son in his sister's room helping her with her snow pants. Not wanting to disturb them she stood in the doorway watching. When her daughter finally had her pants on, she snuck across the hall and into her room.

Quietly she closed the door and when she turned around, she caught a glimpse of her husband's bare chest as he was pulling his sweatshirt over his head. 'My...my...my,' she thought to herself as she stared at his rippled chest, 'what a lucky woman I am.' She then made her way closer towards her husband.

When Sean finally managed to get his head through the sweatshirt, he was somewhat startled to see his wife standing in front of him. "Cassandra, I didn't hear you come in."

"That's ok," said Cassandra as she slinked in a little closer. Feeling a little flirtatious she slid her hands under his sweatshirt. She then began rubbing her fingers against his chest and lowered her voice, "I was just admiring you."

Sean raised his head and couldn't help but moan as his wife's fingertips found their way around his nipples giving him goose bumps. As his blood began to boil within, he reached out and placed his hands upon her hips hoping she would stop. But when she didn't, he gazed down at her with the same smirk he had worn in the kitchen and in a smooth husky voice he said, "You know this is not going to work."

"Are you sure?" Cassandra then raised herself up on her toes. When she was at the right height she began to lick his earlobe.

Tilting his head to the side and closing his eyes, another moan escaped his lips, "Ohhh...that's working, but...ah...oh...that's not what I meant."

Just then a knock came to the door and the voices of their children broke the spell.

"That's what I meant." Sean sighed.

"Oh pooh," Cassandra huffed. Disappointed, she lowered her feet back onto the floor while at the same time pulling her hands out from her husband's sweatshirt.

Surprised how quickly his wife gave up Sean made one more promise before letting her go. "Keep that thought and tonight after the kids are tucked in, we will act on it."

When her husband moved his hands, away Cassandra playfully giggled as she batted her eyelashes. Feeling good about what was yet to come, she made her way to the bedroom door and opened it. There in the hallway stood her two prized possessions dressed in their thick snow pants and long-sleeved warm shirts just waiting to be taken out into the abundant snow they had been blessed with. Nonetheless, no matter how eager they were she was amazed at how well the two remembered their manners and did not try to rush past her to hurry their father along. Instead, the two little darlings stayed planted almost quietly awaiting their father to join them. As she continued holding the door she looked down at them and noticed they both were slightly twitching their heads. She moved her eyes towards the direction they were motioning to, and all of a sudden, she realized she was still in her pajamas. Now she understood what her children were telling her. Politely without words they wanted her to get dressed. By now her husband had finished dressing and joined them at the door. Then he too hinted about her state of dress. "Ok...ok, I get it. I'll just take a minute or two."

Sean wrapped one arm around his wife's waist and placed a peck on her cheek. "Good. I'll finish getting Elicia ready and take her with us out to the garage. You can meet up with us there." After releasing her waist, he took hold of his children's hands and led them away.

After closing the door behind them Cassandra hurried over to the closet and started pushing hangers out of the way. She needed to find a warm dry shirt to wear under her jacket. Since it was Christmas, she was on a mission to find one shirt in particular. It was a green long-sleeved turtleneck with three holly leaves and red berries embroidered on the neck. This shirt was the very first Christmas present her husband had bought for her after they had gotten married. As she slid the hangers down the clothing rod, she finally laid her eyes upon it. Before yanking it off the hanger she lightly touched the fabric and ran her fingers down the sleeve. She began to feel bad she had not worn it more often. But this year was different and in order to show her husband how much she appreciated all he was doing for her she was bound and determined to wear it.

Carefully she pulled the shirt off the hanger and draped it over her arm. After closing the closet door, she walked over and laid it gently across the bed. Now she had to find some thermal underwear to wear underneath. She stepped over to her dresser and pulled open the top drawer. Being organized the drawer held all her matched socks on one side while the other held her folded undergarments. And in the middle, she divided the sides with her bras. But hidden towards the back where she kept her small stack of night garments, she knew she would find what she was looking for.

She began lifting up each piece carefully so not to unfold anything. When she got close to the bottom, she found a two-piece set of pink thermal undergarments and pulled them out. After tossing them onto the bed she grabbed a bra before closing the drawer.

With the necessary clothing all laid out Cassandra sat on her side of the bed and began trading her pajama bottoms for the thermal ones. When she had the bottoms snug up to her waist, she went about pulling her arms out of her sleeves, but before lifting it over her head she clasped her bra around her chest and pulled the straps over her shoulders. To keep from getting cold she quickly exchanged the night top for the thermal shirt.

Only one slight shiver made it past her attempt to stay warm as she picked up the green Christmas turtleneck lying next to her. Before putting it on she stood in front of the antique mirror that stood between her side of the bed and the dresser. As she gazed at herself in the mirror, she held the shirt in front of her and remembered the very first Christmas they had spent as husband and wife.

It was early morning, and the two lonely gifts looked huge against the small tabletop tree. They each picked up their gift for the other and at the same time exchanged them. After they tore through the wrapping she held in her hand a long white rectangle gift box. Eager to see what was inside, she lifted up the lid. Inside under the white tissue paper was the green turtleneck. When she looked up her husband was smiling with two ski tickets in his hand.

A sigh of contentment escaped her lips as she reminisced of the joy and love they shared with one another that day, and every day since. Holding onto that feeling, she finally put it on and was surprised it still fit. Pleased with knowing how happy she was going to make her husband she went into the bathroom where her snow pants had been hung up to dry. As she reached up to grab her pants she quickly glanced at her watch and was amazed at how much time had already flown by. Her thoughts reverted to how much more she still needed to do before she would be ready for company. Hurriedly she slipped on her pants then zipped them up. Next, she made her way back over to the dresser and grabbed a clean pair of heavy socks from the top drawer before heading to the garage.

By the time Cassandra finally joined her family, her husband and son had already had the garage door opened and the snowplow running. As she stood on the steps it looked to her as if they were already making some headway with one half of the driveway. But then she noticed her daughter just standing on the edge of the garage alone. Suddenly a chill ran through her and she remembered she had forgotten her jacket, so she scurried back inside and grabbed her jacket off the hook in the entryway then quickly rejoined her daughter, this time by her side. "Hey, are you ready to go make some snow angels?"

"Oh, yes mommy!" Elicia grinned from ear to ear. "I'm ready."

Before stepping out of the garage Cassandra took some time to search for the perfect place to begin their quest. She first glanced to her right but the added snow from the snowplow made the bank at least a foot higher than the other side that had not been cleared yet. There would be no way her daughter could even walk through that high of snow. And for her to carry her daughter was out of the question. Still, not wanting to disappoint her she took hold of her hand and decided they would try and walk through the two feet of snow on the other side.

Carefully and cautiously, she guided her daughter out onto the slick pavement. She was busy concentrating on every step when suddenly her foot slid slightly. She stopped to regain her balance. As she stood there, she feared she would have to make an unfavorable decision and go back on her deal. But after a moment she decided to give it one more chance. Before pressing on she looked up and noticed her husband was trying to catch her attention.

Above the sound of the machine, she could not make out what her husband was saying but noticed he kept pointing off to his right. Since that was the same direction, they had already chosen, she just acknowledged him and once more put her attention to the dangerous pavement in front of her. After a few more steps she felt, her hand being yanked indicating to her that her daughter had begun to slip and slide. She quickly turned around and grabbed firmly onto her daughter's arm with her other hand in order to keep her upright. "You ok, Icia?"

"Ah hum," answered Elicia when she finally got both of her feet planted back on the pavement.

"Are you sure you still want to do this?" No answer was necessary when those blue eyes met with hers. Then in the distance she heard her husband's voice and looked up. When she noticed the sound of the machine had stopped, she yelled, "What?"

"We dug you a path. Just a few feet further."

Cassandra and her daughter were off once more, only this time she held onto her arm with a firmer grip. They walked almost halfway down the driveway when just as her husband said, she could see a wide opening large enough for the two of them to walk through. To her astonishment he had also left at least three inches of snow on the ground to give them better traction. At least that was what she believed until the two of them made their way to a wider opening that had purposely been dug out low enough so they could make their snow angels without becoming buried within the snow. Warmed by the thoughtfulness of her husband and son, she eyed the area then looked down at her daughter. "Did you know about this?"

"Yes Mommy."

"Why didn't you tell me?"

Elicia's face just lit up as she giggled then said, "Silly Mommy, you didn't ask."

With that her daughter broke away from her and ran into the open space.

The Invitations

Lying down in the snow Cassandra had been swishing her arms above her head when a shadow appeared above her. With the haze of the winter sun glaring down into her eyes she could only make out who or what it was. As she squinted her eyes to block some of the glare the shadow transformed into the shape of a man. Before she could raise her hand to cut out more of the glare, he leaned over to help her. She was then able to catch a glimpse of his face and realized it was someone she held dear to her heart. "I thought you weren't coming."

"I would never leave you."

Overwhelmed with joy Cassandra reached up and grabbed her brother's arm. She then pulled down forcing him to kneel. With him now by her side she asked, "Is everyone here?" Her question was soon followed by a low chuckle and her smile abruptly faded.

"Honey, I haven't invited anyone yet."

Shocked, the voice did not belong to her brother she quickly released him. After raising her hand to cut out the rest of the glare she took a better look at his face. "Sean?"

"Well, you haven't given me a set time yet. So, I figured before Ronnie, and I venture out to save our neighbors I would ask." Sean stood back up then leaned over and offered his hand. "I didn't want to make two trips."

Before accepting his help Cassandra sat up for a moment wondering if she was ever going to stop hearing voices. But now she had begun to see things and she knew this was not good. If only she could mention this to her husband, but she knew if she did, he would only give her excuses. No, for now, she would keep this to herself. Finally, she reached out a hand to meet his'. When she was back on her feet, she brushed the snow from her clothing and answered her husband's question, "Two thirty."

"Two thirty it is then." Sean turned to walk away but remembered his son's request, so he turned back around. "Ah, before Ronnie and I venture out to the street could you make us some hot chocolate to warm us up?"

"Sure."

"Thanks, we'll meet you at the front door. I still need to finish shoveling the front walkway." Before leaving Sean placed his hands upon his hips and surveyed the area. By the looks of things, he could tell it was going to take most of the morning to dig out his neighbors. However, it was well worth the time and trouble if it made his wife happy. "Well, I guess we better get going if we're going to get the invitations out in time."

As her husband walked off Cassandra raised her hand and placed it on her forehead, nothing. She lowered her hand somewhat disappointed for secretly she had hoped she was coming down with something, and that would explain why she was hearing and seeing things. On the other hand, she was relieved because she still had to get things ready. With a time now set for dinner she glanced around the area for her daughter. At first glance she could not see her. But then she thought she saw a chunk of snow shoot upward then plop back down. When she heard a faint giggle, she carefully made her way through the snow towards the sound. She was almost there when her daughter popped up out of the snow.

"Mommy!" called out Elicia. She then stretched her arms out in front of her wanting to be picked up.

After picking up her daughter and placing her on her hip, Cassandra lightly tapped her nose and stated, "You, young lady, look like you are cold."

"A little," Elicia answered through slightly chattering teeth. "I think I got some snow down my coat."

"Oh, in that case maybe we should get you inside so you can dry off." Cassandra crunched her way back through the snow in the same direction from where they had entered. This time the path seemed lower and shorter. It looked like her husband and son had finished with the driveway and laid down some rock salt to keep it from becoming slippery. Even though she knew the rock salt would help she did not want to take any chances. She lowered her daughter to the ground and took hold of her hand. Before stepping out she placed her boot onto the pavement and shuffled it back and forth making sure she had some traction. When her boot jerked more times than slid, she continued on with the other. More at ease with her progress, she tugged slightly on her daughter's hand instructing her to follow.

Slowly they made their way up the driveway and to the opened garage. Once they were safely inside Cassandra patted her daughter on the back to usher her into the house. As her daughter obeyed, she peeked around the corner of the garage door back outside. She watched as her two men bustled to get the front walk ready for company. They were already one quarter of the way to the steps, and she knew she had to hurry in order to get their coco ready. Quickly she walked across the garage floor and turned the knob that led inside.

As the dining room came into view so did the pile on the floor. Crumpled up beside the door lay the outside clothing her daughter had been wearing just moments before, but where was she? Cassandra took in a light sigh as she bent over to pick up the pile and spoke to herself, "A mother's work is never done." Unfortunately, once she had the clothing in hand, she noticed that the floor was now wet. It seemed her missing daughter had a lot more snow left on her than she originally thought. As she eyed the puddle, she soon found the watery tracks that would eventually lead her to her daughter. The wet footprints led from the garage door and through the kitchen, 'at least she was smart enough to stay off the carpet,' she thought to herself. Then as the trail ended, she spotted her daughter sitting on the bench in the entryway trying to peel off her wet socks.

Hearing her mother approach Elicia looked up. "I seem to be having issues," she said as she lifted up her leg. "Can you help me?"

"Of course," Cassandra looked down into her arms at the pile of wet clothing.

"I am sooo sorry mom," Elicia stated as she watched and waited while her mother placed her jacket on the hook and hung her pants up next to it.

"That's ok honey. We just need to remember to get a towel from the bathroom to mop up the water on the floor, so no one slips on it." She smiled as she knelt down and began to peel the wet socks off her daughter's feet. When she had them in her hands she stood back up and glanced out the small window on the front door to check on her husband's progress. Much to her surprise she could see them making their way up the steps. "Goodness. Your father and brother are on their way in, and I was supposed to make them some hot chocolate."

"Hurry mom. I'll go get the towel for the floor." Elicia dashed off the bench and ran down the hall.

With her daughter's plan in mind Cassandra quickly went back into the kitchen and grabbed two clean mugs from the dishwasher then filled them with water. She had just placed them into the microwave and set the timer when the front door opened.

"Burrr...it is cold out there," Sean stated as he pulled his gloves off and patted them together. "Is the coco done yet? We could sure use some warmth right now."

"It will just be a minute," Cassandra yelled back.

"I've got the towel." Elicia flew past her father and as she reached the entry of the kitchen, she dropped the towel onto the floor and began mopping up her watery trail.

"Thank you, Icia." Cassandra then heard the microwave go off and quickly went into action. She prepared the drinks for her industrious men as fast as she could without losing any of the love and care she normally put into it. However, as she carried the mugs to them the frozen looks upon their faces told her it did not matter how she made them just as long as they were made. "Here, drink this. It will put warmth in your tummies and the color back to your faces."

Ronnie cupped his hands around the warm mug and quietly said, "Ah...this feels good." He then stuck out his tongue and licked the top of his whip cream off.

"Here is yours." Cassandra handed her husband the other mug without whip cream.

Even though his cheeks were red Sean's face felt very cold because the wind had begun to pick up outside and numbed his face. But now that he was inside, he could feel the sting. In order to help bring the feeling back he held the mug against his cheeks for a moment. When he could finally feel the warmth, he lowered the mug to his mouth and took a sip. "Oh yeah, I really needed that."

Cassandra stood with her arms tucked under her breast watching her men enjoy the warmth from their hot liquids. Then a thought popped into her mind, so she had to ask, "Are you both riding on the snowplow, or is Ronnie going to walk behind you with the wagon and shovel to lay down the rock salt?"

Sean was in the middle of another sip when he looked down at his son. He knew Ronnie would do anything he asked without complaint. But this was no ordinary snow fall. It would take them a while before they would be able to complete their mission. So, Sean decided to go with his initial rule for his son's safety. "Ronnie will ride up with me. I'm sure I can rig the plow to spray out the rock salt behind us. That way it would cut our time in half. Besides, I'm going to need him to go up to the neighbors' doors in order to invite them. Is that ok with you?"

Noticing his father was speaking to him, Ronnie looked up from his mug and answered with a smile.

"Ok then. I will make the two of you a thermos of hot chocolate. Now finish those and I'll meet you in the garage." Cassandra went back into the kitchen and began her search for the big thermos they used for their picnics.

Meanwhile, Sean and his son finished their drinks and decided to take the short cut to the garage. As they made their way through the kitchen they heard a small voice scream at them.

"I just mopped that." Frustrated Elicia stood up and threw her towel down onto the floor. She then turned to her mother and asked, "Mom! I don't have to clean up after them too. Do I?"

Looking down at his feet Sean realized they had tracked mud and snow from their boots onto the floor. And by the look on his daughter's face and the towel lying next to her he could tell that she had just wiped the floor and was in no mood to do it again. "Sorry sweetie. Maybe your mother will help out?"

Luckily for Cassandra her husband had not quite gotten out of her reach, so she swung her arm out hitting him with the backside of her hand. "Why can't you clean up after your own mess?"

"Ouch!" Sean let out as he stopped to rub his arm.

"Elicia, don't worry about it for now. I will deal with it after I fix this thermos for your father and brother," answered Cassandra as she gave her husband a stern frown. She then had an idea and turned to her daughter to ask, "Would you like to help me?"

"Would I!" Elicia made her way past her father and brother to join her mother by the sink. "What would you like me to do?"

While the males of the family exited out the garage door Cassandra went over to the dining room to collect a chair and carried it over to the sink for her daughter to stand on. She knew how important it was to involve her daughter in every step even if she was too young to do it. When her daughter was in the seat, she bent down and took out a saucepan from the cabinet next to her and placed it into the sink. Next, she had her daughter turn on the faucet. "Elicia, can you do me a favor?"

"Sure."

"Will you watch the water and turn it off when the pan is three quarters of the way full. That way I can clean up your father's mess off the floor before it dries."

"Ok." Elicia stared into the saucepan watching the water rise.

With her daughter now busy Cassandra went over and grabbed the towel from the floor. She then dropped to her knees and with the towel she rubbed it across the linoleum in front of her. When that spot was cleaned, she scooted across the floor making her way through the kitchen towards the entryway. It didn't take long to wipe up all the mud and, in the end, she held up the towel. For the first time she noticed it was, or it used to be white. What was her daughter thinking when she picked out this towel from all the others to mop the floor with? Well, it was too late the damage had been done and now the white had turned into a dingy brown. Holding onto the towel between her fingertips she stood up and carried it to the washer in the garage.

Inside the garage Cassandra walked over to the washing machine and lifted the lid. After tossing the towel inside she closed the lid and turned to find her husband's head under his monstrous machine while her son knelt down beside him with a toolbox in hand. Not wanting to disturb them she went back into the house to check on her daughter.

"There you are. I've been waiting for you." Elicia looked at her mother while she still stood upon the chair where she had been left. "The pan is ready."

"Good." Cassandra joined her daughter then reached into the sink and grabbed hold of the handle with both hands. "Do you want to help me put this on the stove?"

"Yes."

"Ok. Place your hands on top of mine. That's good. Now when I count to three, we'll lift the pan out and move it over towards me." Cassandra hoped the weight of the water would not be too much for them. "One...two...three...lift."

Elicia held onto her mother's hands as tightly as she could, trying hard not to let go. It felt good her mother needed her help, and she so wanted to be a part of all the festivities. However, the pan began to wobble as they lifted it from its resting place, and she was not sure if she would be able to hold on. "Mom..."

"We're almost there, just a little further." Cassandra could feel her daughter's hands begin to slip off of hers. Just when she thought she was going to lose her the pan was right over the spot she wanted, and they lowered it onto the burner. "See, you did it."

"I did." Elicia was happy that she had not given up and now she had accomplished her first step in cooking. "What's next?"

Cassandra giggled at the excitement and enthusiasm her daughter showed. It seemed now that she had her first taste of cooking there was nothing stopping her from wanting to learn more. This pleased her because she had been waiting to have someone, she could share her passion with. "Well, I need to turn on the burner so the water will boil."

"Can I do that?"

"Ok." Cassandra picked her daughter off of the chair and held her over the stove. "See the first knob on your left?"

"Yeah."

"I want you to push it in and turn it towards the others until the line is at the bottom." Cassandra watched as her daughter reached out and with her tiny, long fingers grabbed hold of the knob and turned it clockwise to the spot she had indicated. She then pulled her daughter back in towards her and lowered her to the floor. "Very good, you are a wonderful helper."

"Thank you. What's next?" Elicia smiled at her mother.

"Now we wait." Cassandra knew she had to check on the turkey, but she did not want her daughter in the way. She had to devise a plan to keep her busy. Her mind whirled through many thoughts. She had to remember that what ever she came up with it had to be believable in order to make her feel important. When she gazed at her watch it was now after ten o'clock. She had less than four and a half hours left before the dinner party. Then it hit her. She had a splendid idea, and the project would keep her busy long enough so she could do what she needed and then some. She then leaned over and said, "I have an important project for you to do. Are you up for it?"

"Sure. What is it?"

"I need you to make the invitations for our neighbors." She looked into her daughter's eyes and could see the wheels turning inside. The light that had shown brightly was now fading with each turn. "Icia, I will help you get started."

"Really?" Elicia perked up.

"Yes. I will write out what you need to put on the card and all you have to do is copy it. Does that sound all right with you?" Cassandra cupped daughter's chin in her hand.

"Can I color pictures on the front?"

"By all means, make them your own." Cassandra released her daughter's chin and took hold of her hand. She then led her into the playroom where she knew they would find the color paper and crayons she would need to make the special cards. As they entered her daughter darted towards the old school desk while she looked around for a pair of safety scissors and a bottle of glue just incase her daughter decided to do more than color. When she spotted the items she needed, sitting on a shelf next to the bookcase, she made the decision to first ask her daughter if she would like to have them. When her daughter told her no, she went over to help her carry the pad of color paper and box of crayons back into the dining room.

Once she had her daughter settled, she wrote what she wanted the invitations to say. It was short and to the point. This would make it easy for her daughter to copy and it read,

Holiday Dinner

2:30pm

Nothing more needed to be said for her husband and son would get the RSVPs when they delivered them. Now she had the freedom to check on the turkey.

Cassandra leaned over with the oven door open and after lifting the lid from the roasting pan the aroma from the turkey escaped hitching a ride along with the steam to engulf any object it came in contact with while on its journey upward. The smell of seasoned stuffing took its toll upon Cassandra's senses and soon she found herself reminded of the day her mother had let her help cook the Christmas meal for the first time.

She was about the same age as her daughter when her mother asked her to join in along with her sister and help prepare the meal that would serve not only them, but their Aunts, Uncles, Cousins and Grandparents as well. To her it was the right of passage and a way to prove her worth in the family. Even though she had been given only the smallest of jobs, like arranging the snack trays and folding napkins, it still made her feel as if she was important and part of the family. Now here she was a mother herself with a daughter she could pass on her traditions too. She was smiling to herself while basting the turkey when she heard her daughter yell.

"The water!"

Startled Cassandra dropped the baster into the pan as she glanced up. Sure enough, the water on the stove had begun to boil over. She quickly retrieved the baster from the pan and replaced the lid. She shoved the turkey back into the oven and closed the door before reaching over to turn off the burner. When the water returned to a simmer, she picked up the pan and moved it over to another burner that was not in use, then gratefully turned to her daughter and said, "Thank you."

"You're welcome. Do you want me to come and help you mix up the chocolate?" Elicia asked as she began to slide off of her chair.

Cassandra knew how much her daughter wanted to help out in the kitchen, but she was now in the middle of something else. "Not this time sweetie, you have a very important job to finish if we want to give them to your father on time."

"Ok." Elicia climbed her way back into her chair. Then lifting up one of the cards she had completed she asked her mother, "Want to see what I have done so far?"

"Sure." Cassandra put down the hot chocolate packets and went over to see. When she reached her daughter, she took the pink piece of folded up colored paper out of her hand. The front bared an awkwardly shaped Christmas tree with brightly colored bulbs. When she flipped the paper opened her daughter had copied exactly what she had written for her. "It's perfect. Now can you make the rest like this one?"

Elicia smiled at her mother and asked, "Yes, but do they have to be the same color?"

Cassandra handed back the invitation to her daughter and answered, "No they can be any color you want them to be."

"Good, 'because I've already made this one blue." Elicia lifted up the one she had hidden underneath the pad of colored paper with a white snowman on the front. "How many more do we need?"

Looking upward in thought Cassandra began counting the houses down their street. Luckily for her their street was a dead end and each house was separated by an acre or two. Then with the help of her fingers she assigned each one the last name of each neighbor starting with the one closest to them on their left. She then circled around until she came back to them. "We'll need about...three. Yes, three more will do."

"Ok. I'm on it."

As her daughter went back to her task Cassandra made her way back to hers. She picked the packages back up off the counter and ripped the envelopes open. Then tilting the opened thermos, she poured in the dry powdery mix. Now came the tricky part. In order not to burn herself while pouring the water from the pan into the small mouth of the thermos she decided to use one of her measuring cups. This process would take longer, but at least she would come out of it unharmed. Cautiously she dipped the measuring cup into the pan then with the thermos tipped towards her over the sink she slowly poured it in with the mixture.

After leaving enough room at the top she screwed the lid back on and shook the thermos until she felt the water and coco had mixed itself inside. With her task done she placed the thermos on the counter then rummaged through the cabinet where she kept the coffee cups. There she found two thermos caps that she had the sense to keep when the thermoses they had belonged to had been long disposed of. With the two metal cups in hand, she gathered the thermos and headed towards the garage door only to stop briefly to check on her daughter, "How's the cards coming?"

"I'm almost done." Elicia glanced up at her mother with her hand still clutching onto a crayon that still rested on the paper. She was in the middle of writing the number two and needed to get back to it, so she quickly finished her answer, "Just one more after this."

"Good. I'll take this to your father and let him know." With her hands full Cassandra placed the thermos under her arm so she could turn the knob on the door to the garage and opened it. From the doorway she could see her husband had just finished wrapping up his handy work on the plow while her son was putting away the tools they had used. Upon entering the garage without her coat Cassandra could feel the chill cut right through her and did not want to stay out there long. She quickly made her way to her husband and handed him the thermos of hot chocolate and the two tin cups. Then before she left, she turned towards her son and asked him to come inside with her for a moment. With her son in tow, she went back inside to see how far her daughter was on the invitations. She leaned over her shoulder and took a glimpse of the creation coming to life on the pink paper.

"Pink trees, blue snowmen," Elicia stated as she picked up a red crayon to draw the circles that would become the bulbs on the tree.

"Well, they look wonderful," Cassandra stated then turned to her son. "When your sister is done with this one, I want you to take these cards and hand them out to our neighbors after you clear their driveways, please."

Ronnie took the ones that were completed from his mother and replied, "Ok."

"I'm going to grab you and your father something to snack on while you are out and about." Cassandra walked over to the refrigerator and searched through the shelves hoping to find something she could fix for a snack. It would have to be something that did not have to be heated because once it was out in the cold it would not hold up well. Then she came across some cheese and sliced summer sausage. This gave her an idea. She grabbed the two items from the refrigerator and along with some crackers she packed them a quick but delicious snack in a sandwich bag. After that she went back to her son and handed him the bag. "Now go to your father and when the two of you get back come let me know who answered yes."

"I will." Ronnie gave his mother a kiss and with the cards and snacks in hand he went back out into the garage to start their chores.

Snacks for All

With everything cleaned up and the boys saving their neighbors Cassandra knew it was time to begin the preparations for the snack trays. She picked up the chair from the sink and placed it in front of the island counter then went to collect the cutting board from behind the toaster. As she carried it over to the counter, she asked her daughter to help gather the things they needed from the refrigerator. Her job would be to grab what she called out and hand it to her to be rinsed off then carry the clean food over to the cutting board. With her instructions understood and her daughter standing with the refrigerator door open, she called out the first vegetable.

Peering downward Elicia tried to remember where her mother had looked the night before for the carrot she gave her for her snowman's nose. She knew it had been somewhere towards the bottom, but they were not on the bottom shelf. Wanting to prove she was capable of doing her new assigned task, she thought really hard to remember. Concentrating on the bottom of the refrigerator she remembered there was a drawer. She glided her hand under the last shelf where she felt the handle then pulled it towards her. There they sat on top of everything else still inside the plastic bag from the store. Happy she had figured it out on her own she grabbed the bag and handed it to her mother.

Looking inside the bag Cassandra wanted to find three of the longest and straightest carrots out of the bunch. She pulled them part way out of the bag one by one until she found three good ones. With the three she wanted set aside she twisted the bag shut and handed the remaining carrots back to her daughter to put away. She then turned on the faucet and one by one she scrubbed the carrots clean using her bare hands. Next, she placed the carrots in a paper towel to be dried off and handed them to her daughter. From there the two of them went over to the cutting board and she helped her daughter up onto her chair. She took the paper towel from her daughter's hands and laid the carrots out onto the cutting board. After grabbing hold of one of the carrots she reached for the knife and cut it in half.

"Aren't you going to peel them first?" asked Elicia for she hoped her mother would peel the outer layer so she could eat them.

"No, the peeling is where most of the vitamins are. If I were to take that away our guest would not get the full benefits from them," Cassandra explained.

A little disappointed Elicia propped up her elbow onto the counter and rested her head in her hand. "You're always thinking of others aren't you mom?"

Cassandra had cut the carrot into eight pieces already and was about to cut each of those pieces in half lengthwise when she noticed her daughter's frown. She then took one of the pieces she had just cut and handed it to her daughter, "Yes. And that also includes you guys."

Elicia's long face turned upwards as her small fingers reached out and accepted the offering, "Thank you."

With her daughter now happy Cassandra was able to continue slicing up the carrots into sticks. When it was completed, she slid the sticks over towards her daughter who in turn picked them up and stuffed them into a large plastic baggy for later. As her daughter carried the bag of carrots back to the refrigerator, she picked up the cutting board and moved it over to the sink to be washed. When it was cleaned and ready for the next vegetable she called out, "Broccoli."

"Got it," Elicia answered after opening up the bottom vegetable drawer. She then handed the bag up to her mother to be washed.

Cassandra placed the broccoli on the counter so she could finish drying off the cutting board. When it was dry she sat the towel down on the counter next to her then placed the cutting board back onto the island counter. She turned back towards the sink and grabbed the broccoli out of the bag. After rinsing it off she shook the broccoli in order to get as much water off as she could. She then placed a paper towel around the stalk to absorb whatever water was left behind before transporting it across the floor to the cutting board. By now her daughter had managed to climb upon the chair herself and was awaiting her next instructions. As she began chopping off the bushy tops, she felt her daughter had become bored, so she suggested for her to go out into the living room and watch some Christmas specials while she finished the veggie tray.

Her daughter declined the offer and once again she wore that glowing smile that always melted her heart. When she thought about it, it was almost like looking into a mirror of herself when she was that age. If only she was young again. Maybe she would be just as excited about new things as her daughter. Then all of a sudden, she realized that even though this was all a routine to her, if she were to look at it through her daughter's eyes she could see and feel the fun and excitement. With that thought in mind she decided to make her daughter a bigger part of the preparations. After she chopped off parts of the broccoli, she scooped them up in her hands and passed them over to her daughter to place in a baggy. As she gathered the stems and sat them back onto the paper towel to be thrown away later, she said, "Elicia I had a thought. Let me run it by you and see what you think."

"Sure." Elicia answered as she bagged the next handful of broccoli tops.

"I was thinking that we could switch rolls this next time around. You can tell me what vegetable you want me to get, and I will hand it to you to wash." Cassandra was in the process of wiping the left-over pieces onto the paper towel with her hand. As she continued to clean off the cutting board she waited for her daughter's answer.

Elicia stood up on the chair holding onto the full bag of broccoli. She wasn't sure if that was all she wanted to do, so she asked, "Does that also mean I get to cut them up?"

As Cassandra carried the unusable parts to the trash, she realized she had not made herself clear about the trade. She took a few seconds to think about her daughter's request while she opened the trash can with her foot and dumped the load in her hands into it. As she stared down into the trash can a flash of reality crossed her mind. She could vividly see her daughter taking hold of the knife and as she cut into the vegetable, she sliced it into one of her fingers. The thought of red spurting out from the wound helped with her decision. "I'm sorry not this time around. Ask me next year."

"It's ok mom. I'm sure you have plenty of other things planned for me today." Elicia handed the bag of broccoli to her mother when she walked up. She then wanted to get ready for her new job and started to climb down from the chair.

"Hang on sweetie, don't get down. I'll just scoot you over to the sink." Cassandra handed the bag back to her daughter and grabbed hold of the back of the chair. She spun it around to face the opposite direction and pushed it across the linoleum floor towards the sink. When the chair was in place she took the bag of broccoli from her daughter and opened the refrigerator placing the bag next to the carrots. Now all she had to do was wait for her daughter to call out what she thought should be next.

"Mushrooms."

Of course, she should have known it would be mushrooms for it was one of her daughter's favorite veggies to dip. As she opened the vegetable drawer she spotted the package of pre-sliced mushrooms. Maybe it was a good thing that she had become lazy over the years with picking out her mushrooms. At least all her daughter had to do was wash them and they were done. Happy about how things worked out she handed the package up to her daughter and closed the drawer along with the refrigerator. She stood beside her daughter watching as her little fingers tried to peel back the plastic wrap that sealed the contents inside.

As her daughter struggled with the wrap Cassandra became nervous and it took all she had to keep from grabbing the package away from her and opening it herself. When the urge became too much to bear, she decided to walk away for a moment to collect the colander from the pantry.

By the time she had returned her daughter had given up on un-wrapping the package from the bottom and was ready to poke her finger into the top. When her daughter's finger went through the plastic, she quickly placed the colander into the sink. She was just in time for the package to fall into it. Wanting to let her daughter figure this out on her own she placed her hands behind her back and waited for her to finish what she had started.

Not detoured, Elicia picked the package back up and finished tearing open the plastic. When it was finally opened, she turned her head and mouthed 'Thank you' as she dumped the mushrooms into the colander.

Knowing very well what she meant Cassandra smiled then lightly whispered back, "You're welcome."

Elicia handed her mother the empty carton then turned on the water. She swirled the colander under the faucet for about fifteen seconds. She then stopped and placed it into the sink to break apart some of them. When they were separated, she picked the colander back up and swirled it around some more. After turning off the water she shook the colander until she felt the mushrooms were dry enough to pour out. "What do I do next?"

Cassandra was way ahead of her daughter and had pulled off two paper towels from the roll on the other side of her. She already had them lying one on top of the other on the counter. "Pour them on here."

Elicia did as her mother said and at the same time tried not to clump them all in one spot. She then used her fingers to scrape the rest of the mushroom off the sides of the colander before placing it into the sink. Her mother then handed her two more sheets to place on top of the mushrooms and told her to pat them lightly to help them dry. When they were done, she carefully peels off the top sheets and watched as her mother packed them into a plastic bag for later. "This is fun mom. What else do we have left?"

"Well let's see. We have carrots, broccoli and now mushrooms. I guess all we have left to do is the cauliflower and cucumbers," answered Cassandra as she placed the mushrooms next to the other pre-sliced vegetables. She then pulled out the vegetable drawer once more and when she looked down, she remembered something else. "Oh, and celery, but I think we are going to put cheese spread on those and put them on a different tray."

"That sounds yummy." Elicia rubbed her stomach and licked her lips at the thought of it. When her mother held up the last two vegetables, she focused back on the current decision. "How about I wash the cucumber, and you do the cauliflower."

"I think that's a fine idea," Cassandra stated as she leaned into the refrigerator and put back the cauliflower. She handed the cucumber to her daughter and waited while she washed it. Being the simplest thing to wash it didn't take long and before she knew it, she was handing her daughter a paper towel. Afterwards she had her daughter hold onto the chair as she pushed it back over to the other counter where she took the cucumber and began to slice it into thin pieces. Then with the knife she scooted the finished product towards her daughter who could not resist snagging one for herself. She heard her daughter giggle and looked over to find her stuffing the piece into her mouth.

This was definitely turning out to be a fun morning for the two of them. Yet, curious about how the boys were doing on their adventure, she quickly finished with the cucumber and left her daughter to bag them as she went over to the window to see if she could see them. She glanced out the window towards the street and even though she could not see their figures she knew it was them. The snow hurled into the air only to land over the curb making a huge pile upon the sidewalk. Content knowing her husband's upgrades on his machine seemed to be working, she turned back in time to switch with her daughter and prepare the cauliflower.

Time was moving right along as they wrapped up preparing all the different foods for the different snack trays minus a few. Nonetheless, she managed to find time to baste the turkey and check its temperature. It was now one thirty and time for her to take the lid off the roasting pan and lower the temperature of the oven. As she dealt with the turkey, she sent her daughter into the dining room with a sponge and a clean towel to make sure the table was clean.

When she had completed the changes to the turkey she made her way over to the china cabinet in the dining room. She opened the top drawer that held the tablecloths and pulled out the red one. Wanting to add more color to the table she also grabbed the green runner to go down the center. After setting the runner on one of the chairs she asked her daughter to come and help her with the tablecloth.

The two of them unfolded the tablecloth until it covered every inch of the dining table leaving enough room to hang slightly over the edge. Now it was time for the runner. Since her daughter could not reach the middle, she had to do this one on her own. She took the runner from the chair and after unfolding it she rolled it up. Now came the tricky part. She leaned over until her eyes were at the same level as the table. When she had herself centered, she placed the rolled-up runner onto the table. As she held on tight to one end, she nudged the other and watched it unroll straight down the center. When it stopped, she took a step away from the table to make sure the runner was indeed in the right spot. She was pleased how well it turned out but then realized there was still one more thing missing from the table.

Allowing her daughter to follow closely behind her, she made her way to the hall closet. There she knew she would find the center piece her mother had given her when she had moved away from home. After opening the door, she pulled out the big box that once held, and would again, the Christmas tree decorations. As her daughter stood beside her she opened the box. Inside amongst the empty boxes of lights and bulbs sat a small box unopened just waiting to be pulled out from its lonely darken home. Carefully she reached in and gently picked up the box. As she pulled out the box, she looked over at her daughter who now stood with her hands out. Before placing the box into her hands she said, "This is a family heirloom, so you will need to hold onto it with both hands."

Elicia understood and nodded her head. She did not want to ruin her chances of helping her mother. So instead of heading back into the dining room she decided to wait. As she waited, she could not help but stare at the box she held in her hands. Maybe some day her mother would hand it down to her. She didn't ponder on the thought for long for she was satisfied with being given the honor to carry this prized procession to its temporary home. When her mother tapped her on the shoulder she gripped tighter to the box and slowly began to walk.

As her daughter led them towards the dining room Cassandra couldn't help but cross her fingers and hold her breath. She knew her daughter was being careful but for some reason she couldn't help how she felt. By the time they reached the table her nerves were on edge, so she motioned for her daughter to pass the box up to her for safekeeping. She waited as her daughter grabbed one side of the chair and slid it slightly away from the table. Then after she climbed onto it, she sat the box down onto the table and moved the chair back in place. When she was positioned right, she picked the box back up then placed it in front of her daughter. She then stepped back behind her and grabbed onto the back of the chair. Her daughter soon turned her head and gave her a questioning look. As she looked back at her she stated, "I'm going to let you open the box this year."

"Really," Elicia was so excited that after her mother confirmed her answer, she drew in a deep breath then turned back around. After letting out her breath she looked down. Not wanting to damage the box or the contents inside she shook her arms to relax. When she felt more at ease she took in one more breath and slowly let it out. With her hands now steady she placed one on each side then with her thumbs she tucked them under the seam. Slowly she raised her thumbs until the lid lifted up. When it popped open, she cried out, "I did it. I opened the box without ripping it."

"That indeed you did. Now I will help you take the piece out." Cassandra released the grip she had on the chair and reached around both the chair and her daughter to grab hold of the box. "I'll hold down the box while you lift the center piece out."

As soon as her mother had a hold of the box Elicia slid her hands out from underneath. Unsure of what would happen she pulled her hands close to her body and asked, "What if I drop it? Are you going to get mad?"

"I know you can do this. Just take one hand and scoop it under...yes like that. Now do the same with the other on this side. Perfect...ok, now clamp your thumbs over the top for a better hold...and lift." Cassandra closed her eyes as her daughter pulled the delicate piece out of the box. When she reopened them, her daughter had already gently placed the tissue wrapped center piece on the table in front of her. She then moved the box to the side and re-gripped the back of the chair. This time she squeezed so tight that her knuckles turned white. She watched with anticipation as her daughter rolled the tissue off, all the while praying her daughter would not break the precious heirloom. When it came out in one piece she sighed with relief. Now relaxed she came around to the side of the chair and smiled at her daughter. "Good job."

"Can I please get down now?"

Cassandra was taken back at her daughter's request. She thought for sure she would want to be able to pick the place to put it. Yet here she was asking to leave, though politely. Not understanding the change in her mood, she took her hands and scooped up her daughter from under her arms then raised her up into the air. "Yes, you may. But can I ask you why?"

"Well, I know I can't reach that far across the table. So instead of being in your way I thought I would move."

Content with the answer Cassandra lowered her closer to her face. She then gave her a noozle before lowering her to the floor. With her daughter behind her she picked up the center piece and held it up to admire.

The white snow-covered country house made out of porcelain had been painstakingly hand painted. Each window shutter had fine details right down to the wood grain in each piece of wood to make it look real. Then there was the string of lights along the roof that hung in blue, red, yellow and green with just a touch of frost to make them twinkle. Even the snow-covered yard had its tall pine trees along with a pile of firewood stacked next to the house. But the artwork she liked the most was the front living room window with the curtains drawn back to allow the viewer to see the family inside toasting the holiday. As she stared into the painted scene her mind drifted and soon, she found herself in complete darkness.

Darkness Descends

Further and further Cassandra descended into a place void of all light. She tried blinking a few times to see if it would help. Unfortunately, that was the problem she couldn't see. Once she realized her vision was gone, she tried to take a breath to calm her nerves, but something felt very wrong. It was as if her ribs were squeezing around her lungs making it hard for her to breathe. Afraid she fumbled her hands around in front of her. When she felt the chair, she clamped her hands down tightly around the back of it. The longer she stood there the tighter her chest became and the more each breath became shorter. Soon her head began to feel light, and she couldn't stop what was happening.

What was going on? Why was this happening to her and why now? Her thoughts raced as panic swept over her. Still gripping onto the back of the chair she closed her eyes and shook her head hoping it would all just go away. Then all of a sudden, her stomach felt queasy and her body heavy. Realizing she was only making matters worse she stopped. As her head continued to spin, she prayed the force of gravity would give up and allow her to stand. Winning at least one of the battles, she opened her eyes only to find she still could not see. Disappointed, she glided her hands down the side of the chair until she found the cushion and sat down. With her body still squeezing the breath out of her she opened her mouth to call out for her daughter. But only a faint whisper escaped her lips, and her call was left unanswered.

The darkness that had descended upon her only deepened with the fear of being alone. In order to stay calm she made herself believe her daughter had gone into the living room to watch some Christmas specials and would be back soon. With that little bit of hope in mind she sat back and prayed it would not take long for her daughter to reappear.

As she sat waiting, she noticed there were no other sounds except her breathing. How could her house be in complete silence when she knew the television was on? There had to be other sounds unless her daughter had turned off everything and went to play in her bedroom. If that were the case, she knew it might be a while before her daughter would reemerge. Deep down she knew her daughter would come back soon, so she listened for the sounds of footsteps heading in her direction.

Seconds turned into minutes and minutes turned into what seemed like an eternity as she sat waiting. Still nothing managed to penetrate the lonely darkness that had engulfed her surroundings. She continued to wait all the while taking shallow breaths and telling herself that someone, anyone would soon pass her way. As more time slipped by, she realized her daughter was too busy playing with her new toys to even think of checking on her. Then out of the blue she finally heard the snowplow outside. Unfortunately, it meant her husband and son were still working and would not be in soon. Now she knew for sure her daughter was her only hope. With that knowledge she became tired of waiting.

Slowly she placed one hand on the table and the other onto the seat of the chair. She then braced for the pain she knew would come as she carefully raised herself up. Unable to stand straight she wrapped one arm around her chest while she used the other to feel her way around. With each step she stopped momentarily because the pain proved to be almost paralyzing. However, she was bound and determined to make it to her daughter, so she attempted to take more steps. Finally, she could feel the difference between the linoleum and the carpet. But then without warning her legs gave out and soon she found her body dropping towards the floor fast with no way of stopping it.

As Cassandra's eyes fluttered, she felt a throbbing pain in her head and couldn't remember what had happened. After awhile she felt the carpet underneath her cheek. She opened her eyes only to find she was surrounded by darkness. It was then she remembered falling to the floor. But how long had she been lying there and why had no one found her? She tried to replay what she had observed before ending up on the floor.

Her husband and son were outside plowing the snow for their neighbors, so that explained why they had not noticed her. But she could not figure out where her daughter had gone. Needing to find help she slowly slid her arms under her chest. Then with all the strength she could muster she pushed her chest away from the floor. She only managed to raise herself up about an inch when the pain proved to be too much, and she collapsed back down onto the floor.

Alone and afraid tears began to escape the corners of her eyes. The next thing she knew she drifted off. As she lay there in the cold darkness, she thought she heard whispering in the distance. She knew opening her eyes wouldn't make a difference, so she kept them closed hoping it would help her hear well as she tried to listen in on the conversation.

The distant whispers soon became louder. Still the voices remained mumbles more than words. Yet, there was one voice in particular that puzzled her. 'No, it couldn't be' she thought to herself. Out of all the people she had hoped to hear this was not one of them. By now it did not matter who it was as long as someone had finally found her. So, with a sigh of joyous relief, she opened her eyes. Unfortunately, the darkness still prevailed so she tried to call out, "Is that you?"

"I'm right here," a female voice answered.

Cassandra's prayers had been answered and someone had finally found her. When she felt the warmth from the hand touching hers, she felt safe at last. But she could not feel the carpet against her face. Was she no longer on the living room floor? With her head still pounding she slowly turned her head. She managed to get a slight grin when her cheek felt the soft cool cotton from the pillowcase underneath. But how did she end up in bed? The question flew out of her head as soon as she heard her mother sigh. She moved her head back and tightened her fingers around her mother's hand. If only she could see her. Knowing it wasn't possible right now she settled for hearing her voice and holding her hand. "I'm so glad you are here."

"So am I."

As she laid in her bed content her thoughts drifted more towards how her husband was able to surprise her. And if her mother was able to get through the snow for Christmas maybe the rest of her family did. Holding onto the hope it was true she turned her head towards her mother and asked, "Is everyone here?"

"Yes dear. They are here."

Relieved, Cassandra closed her eyes, but the pounding in her head would not subside. By now she could also feel the pain throughout her entire body making it unbearable to rest. She was just about to ask her mother for some relief, when she felt something cool enter her veins. Not long afterwards she began to feel nothing but sleepiness. Her mind began to spin, and she found it harder to collect her thoughts. She still had so many questions to ask but only managed, "Mom, how did you get through the snow?"

"Oh sweetie, I'm not sure I understand."

"There is about three feet just out front." With her mind racing and her thoughts jumbled, Cassandra thought for a moment about her own question. When she realized her husband must have cleared all the snow away, she stated, "Never mind. I'm just glad you are here."

Suddenly the room fell into an awkward silence. With her mind not functioning properly Cassandra tried to figure out what she had said wrong. As she picked her brain for the answer she began to hear mumbled whispers in the distance. Once again, she found herself straining to hear what was being said. When the mumbling stopped, she heard one pair of footsteps leave the room while another crept closer to her. After a few moments of soft whispers between her mother and a male she felt a pat on the back of her hand.

"Cassandra, dear...you have had a rough morning. Maybe you should rest some more."

"Mom, I don't have time to rest." Cassandra eagerly tried to lift herself up, but the swirling in her head and the hand upon her shoulder stopped her from going very far. Disappointed she pleaded, "Please mom, I still have to finish preparing dinner before everyone arrives. Since I can't see could you help me?"

Cassandra could hear her mother stammering trying to figure out a way to answer her. She couldn't understand why her mother could not give her a straight answer. Before long she heard the door opened, and footsteps approach. When they stopped, she was able to hear what was being said between her mother and the other person.

"It's time to let her rest...," the male started to say until he realized the girl in the bed had her eyes open, "Oh good you're finally awake."

"I think she is blind."

The voices started to fade back into the background leaving Cassandra to wonder what they were saying about her. The further away the voices got the more afraid she became. Frightened she was going to be left alone she reached out to squeeze her mother's hand, but it only slipped away. With tears in her eyes she called out, "Mom...Mom..."

Just as she thought she was completely alone she felt her hair being lightly brushed away from her face with warm fingertips. The light kiss upon her cheek that soon followed made her close her eyes. Knowing someone was still with her allowed her to think upon what her mother had said. How could she be blind? She had done nothing to cause it. And of all the times this could happen this was not a good one. As she laid there feeling sorry for herself the sounds of the world around her began to break through. But out of all of them only one noise in particular brought her out of herself absorbed pity.

"Oh... my... God! The turkey!" The sound of the timer from the stove made Cassandra's eyes pop open and prop up from the bed. Now sitting up, she stopped from getting out of the bed when she realized her pain was gone and so was the dizziness in her head. But there was one more thing that surprised her as she turned her head. There beside her sat her husband. "Sean?"

"I'm right here."

"I can see you." Cassandra raised her hand and placed it lovingly upon his face.

"Of course you can," answered Sean as he took her hand from his face and cupped it into his own.

"No, you don't understand. I can see again."

Concerned about her state Sean gently pushed her back down onto the bed. When her head hit the pillow, he kindly suggested, "I think you need to rest some more."

"But I have to get up and take out the turkey." Determined to fulfill her obligation Cassandra tried to sit back up, but her husband would not allow it and held her down in place.

"Don't worry we have it taken care of." When she stopped struggling Sean reached over to the nightstand to collect the cool damp wash cloth. After folding it he placed it on her forehead. "Now rest. You still have a few more minutes before the rest of our guests are scheduled to arrive."

Relieved her husband had everything under control Cassandra reached up and grabbed hold of the hand his still had on the washcloth. When he squeezed back, she knew he would take care of her. As he lowered her hand back down by her side, she turned her head to face him, and he smiled. She smiled back then waited for him to spring his surprise.

Moments slipped by without any words and the suspense was getting to her. She already knew her mother was there, but she wanted him to tell her. When it became too much to bear, she decided to drop hints to get him to say. "So, who is taking care of the dinner?"

"Mrs. O'Neil," Sean answered.

"Oh," Cassandra let out somewhat disappointed. She then thought maybe he was just trying to keep her off track so he could spring it on her later. So, playing along with the game she asked another question, "Did she have to come a long way to help?"

"No, Ronnie and I were just inviting her when Elicia came running up to the door. After she told us what had happened Mrs. O'Neil naturally volunteered to come over to help."

By now Cassandra thought either he was telling the truth, or he was still trying to hide the fact that her mother was there. Tired of playing the game she raised her other hand from across the bed and placed it upon his forearm. She then looked him straight in the eyes and said, "Where's my mother? I know she is here."

Sean shook his head as he lowered it in bewilderment. He couldn't understand why she thought her mother was there. Maybe she hit her head harder than they originally thought. In any case he knew he needed to get her to understand the truth. So, with a loving hand he placed it on top of hers and raised his head back up. When their eyes met, he stared right into hers and reaffirmed, "Honey she's not here. Remember their flight was cancelled due to the snow."

"Oh God," Cassandra let go of her husband's arm and placed it on the side of her head. "I'm losing it aren't I?"

"No," Sean answered as he lightly brushed her cheek with his fingertips. Then with a gentle smile he stated, "The living room floor was just a little harder than we thought, but don't worry you didn't leave a dent."

As they both found humor in his words Cassandra lowered her hand and brushed it against his as he continued to touch her cheek. It wasn't until then did she realized she must be rubbing off on him for the joke was on her this time. She took a hold of his hand and lowered it to her mouth. With his open palm facing her lips she placed a soft kiss into it. As her eyes began to close, she remembered what she was doing right before everything went black. Even though she did not remember hearing anything break her eyes began to tear up at the mire thought of her family heirloom shattered into tiny pieces. "Sean, be honest with me. Did I break anything when I fell?"

Sean leaned in a little closer to her face for he knew exactly what she was concerned about. "The center piece is fine. We found you in the living room far away from the dining table."

Cassandra was relieved for she wasn't sure if she could trust her own memories anymore. She gave her husband one more kiss in the palm of his hand before he slowly pulled it away.

"Now I must go help the others with Christmas dinner." Sean stood up and after he tugged down on his new sweater he looked back at his wife. "Hey, don't look so glum. Everything will turn out perfectly just as you planned."

"But it's not."

"Look honey, you had everything prepared ahead of time, so don't worry. And when you feel up to it you can come and join us."

Cassandra nodded as she watched her husband walk away then closed the door behind him. Alone again she laid there wondering what was going on with her. Why was she drifting back and forth between what seemed like two worlds? There had to be a logical explanation and the one her husband kept giving her did not seem to fit what she was experiencing. He didn't understand that everything she saw, heard or felt seemed so real. She knew she had to find the answers before she could join the others. So, after turning back over onto her back and placing the cloth over her eyes she allowed herself to welcome in the darkness.

The Journey

As the sounds of the holiday merriment grew outside her door, Cassandra began her walk down the path within her mind. The further away she got from the life she knew, the darker her surroundings became. She continued her long journey in what could only be described as a blackened vas of nothingness. Her stomach began to quiver at the fear of what she might find, so she stopped. As she stood in the eerie silence, she thought about what she hoped to find. If there were answers, would they be enough to satisfy her?

The madness of what she was doing became very clear when heard her husband's sweet voice whispering her name from a distance. As the warm breath from the whisper touched her ear, she remembered what was important in her life. Everything she had ever wanted was back towards the lighted room where she had come from. Without any further thought she turned around to go back.

Before she had a chance to move her right hand automatically raised and cupped her mouth as it dropped open. She could not believe what was happening. The light that would guide her back to her bedroom was slipping away from her and fast. With no time to lose she decided to make a run for it. Unfortunately, her legs felt as if they were moving in slow motion.

Panic soon swept over her as she found herself going nowhere but still racing towards her life. It didn't seem to matter how fast she ran, the light from her room kept getting smaller. Her heart pounded louder against her chest while her breath grew heavy with each step of her feet. She continued to run as fast as she could until there was nothing left to chase, and she had no other choice than to stop.

Quickly she turned in a complete circle hoping there was another sign of light. But to her dismay there was none. Now fully engulfed by the emptiness she wondered how she was going to get to her husband and children. As she pondered upon her situation, she could see her words stream past her. 'How could this be?' one sentence read, and another 'what was that?' The whole thing caught her by surprise at first, but she soon realized it made perfect sense for her to see her thoughts since she was indeed in her own mind. For awhile she continued to watch her thoughts roll by. But eventually she became tired of it and placed her face into her hands. She could no longer bear seeing her own answers to her questions, and prayed whatever brought her here would also take her back.

With her eyes covered she listened intensely to everything around her. She hoped the sounds of Christmas merriment would return followed by the light. However, her hopes were dashed when the only sound she heard was the void of what wasn't. A heavy sigh of defeat escaped her lips as she opened her eyes knowing she still stood inside the darkness of her mind. Finally, she understood she had to continue forward if she wanted to go back.

Slowly she turned upon the floorless space with her arms wrapped around her to fight off the chill. With her direction unknown she turned and turned until she found herself spinning out of control. She stretched out her arms frantically trying to catch something within the darkness that could stop her. Just as she thought there would be no end, she saw what she thought was a small speck of light streak by.

All of a sudden, she stopped spinning, and her body abruptly dropped. Her eyes took some time to stop moving, but once they did, she noticed the light was in front of her. As she stared toward it, it twinkled and danced beckoning her to get up and walk. Though uncertain of what she would find inside the mysterious light she complied and cautiously made her way towards it.

As she began her journey down the darkened path she wondered if this light would soon disappear like the other. Yet something deep inside her carried her onward. Along the way she felt something was changing so she glanced around and noticed slightly discolored circles beginning to form on each side of her. Curious, she steps towards one of the circles on her right and stretches out her hand.

Somewhat afraid of what would happen she hesitated. She then glanced back towards the light. Once she knew it wasn't going anywhere, she turned back towards the circle. With her hand close enough she used her fingertip to touch the center. When she retracted her hand, the circle began to ripple. It soon began to stretch itself into other shapes.

Amazed at the sight, she thought about taking a step back but did not dare. She could not help but watch as the circle turn into an oval then into a rectangle, all the while still rippling as if it were liquid. Transfixed on what was transforming in front of her she continued to watch as the ripples finally came to a stop and turned into something more solid.

A large wooden door soon formed along with its brass knob. Not sure if it was real, she slowly stepped in closer. She then placed her hand against the wood. It was indeed solid. Knowing it was real she lowered her hand and wrapped her fingers around the knob. As soon as she clinched tight, she felt a warm sense of contentment sweep over her. No longer afraid she turned it.

When she opened the door, a bright white light rushed towards her only to vanish as it reached her. After rubbing her eyes and a few blinks she was able to see the back of a dark-haired young man dressed in jeans and a white tee-shirt. She noticed he was standing in the kitchen and had grabbed something off of one of the countertops. Unable to see what it was she watched as he walked away from her. She could tell by his slow pace that he must be carrying something of importance. Intrigued to find out what it was she stood in the doorway holding onto the door.

She watched him walk out from the kitchen when she realized there was something familiar in the way he carried himself. It wasn't until he had reached the end of the table filled with children on each side and turned around that she recognized his face. The corners of her mouth crept upwards into a gentle smile as she watched her father place the cake in front of the blond-haired girl.

What started out as a distant scene soon zoomed in closer, allowing her to see the cake. It was the most beautiful thing she had ever seen. In the middle stood a Barbie doll with a blue icing top that flowed down towards the purple and blue striped covered skirt. If she remembered correctly the inside was made from her favorite flavor, chocolate. She began to lick her lips as she waited in anticipation for what was to come next. Then she saw her father lean over with a lighter in hand. This was it, the big moment. The candles sticking out of the skirt were lit.

As the flames danced, she listened while her father started the birthday song. When the others joined in so did she. With each note she felt the love for her father grow and soon one lonely tear escaped her eye. Unfortunately, everything had an end and so did the song. When it was over she wiped away the water from her cheek and watched the girl with golden blond curls lean over as her father held her hair back.

"Now make a wish, Cassy," he stated.

The smaller version of herself closed her eyes tightly and mumbled quietly under her breath. When her lips stopped moving, she popped her eyes back open and took a deep breath. Then with a little help from her father the two of them blew. The flames flickered from side to side as they fought hard against the winds, but they never stood a chance once the two of them teamed up.

When the last candle was snuffed Cassandra found herself with her lips puckered as if she too were blowing. She knew what she had wished for that eighth birthday. When they began to cut the cake, she unknowingly whispered out loud, "Barbie Town house." As soon as she heard herself, she clapped her hand over her mouth. She looked around the room to see if anyone had heard her and much to her relief no one had. The scene continued to play just the way she had remembered and once the gift she had wished for was opened she decided it was time to leave.

Leaving behind the happiness she once knew she stood in the darkened empty space with only one light to guide her. She turned towards it and continued her journey. This time she noticed the path didn't seem as dark as before. New doors were constantly forming on both sides of her, but when she looked forward the light strangely seemed to stay at a constant distance.

As time went by, she began to have doubts that she was indeed moving. She turned her head towards her left at the only objects that could confirm her movement. When she saw the doors were still passing her by, she wondered if they were moving and not her. Before she had the chance to ponder about it one of the doors caught her attention. It was not like any of the others with its dark almost charcoal like color. Stunned at the discoloration she stopped to investigate.

With her hand she touched the door and found it to be rougher than the last. But that wasn't the only difference. When she grabbed hold of the tarnished knob for some reason it did not give her the same feeling as before. The deep despair she felt made her more curious about what was on the other side. Wanting to know what could cause so much grief she decided to open it.

It was now three years later, and her father lay quietly in a beautifully carved wooden bed surrounded by the emotional wailings of people dressed in the darkest clothing they could find. At eleven she stood alongside her mother not understanding why her father wasn't coming back. Even more confusing was how everyone around them was being so nice.

Now she was older and understood, but it didn't make the loss any easier. She felt the warm stream of tears run down her face as she thought of her father's passing. The pain of losing her father grew as she watched her mother, barely able to walk up the steps to the light wooden coffin. When she spotted her younger self dash towards her mother, she felt a strong urge to go inside. She tried to rush in and comfort herself, but an invisible barrier only allowed her to go for a short distance. When it snapped back it sent her out into the dimly lit path, landing on her rear-end then before she had the chance to get back up the door slammed shut. She now realized she was not allowed to interfere with the past.

Gradually she stood back up and straightened her hair. She could not believe her mind would turn on her like that. Did she not have full control over what happens inside? Needing to find another happier memory to get rid of the pain in her heart she walked over to the next door. This time she would just watch no matter what it revealed.

Without hesitation she grabbed the knob and to her surprise it dissolved in her hand. Thinking the door was not meant to be opened she walked over to another only to have it do the same. Trying to stay calm she made her way to the next. This time as she reached for the knob the door itself began to disappear.

"No...no," Cassandra cried. She quickly looked back from where she had come and noticed nothing but darkness. When she looked ahead the doors in front of her were dissolving. Frantic, she began to run as fast as she could to get ahead of the void before it could completely engulf her. However, just when she thought she was pushing ahead another door vanished beside her, letting her know the darkness was gaining ground. Knowing her only hope was to reach the light she picked up her speed.

Her legs were almost a blur as they tried hard to press forward, but it did not matter how fast she ran the brightness stayed the same. She felt as if she was running in place. Yet, when she glanced behind her she could see the path being devoured by the emptiness. She then knew she had to be heading somewhere, but where?

As the doors continued to vanish Cassandra's body grew tired. There seemed to be no end in sight, and no goal that could be reached. She decided to give up and stop. All the hopes of finding out what was happening to her were dashed in an instant. Needing to catch her breath she leaned over.

With her hands upon her knees and her head facing down she was ready to give into the darkness. As she braced herself for the unknown a warm sensation brushed the side of her. When she looked over, she could see the light coming towards her. The brightness grew larger the closer it became. Even though it showed nothing of what it held inside she heard a deep rumble.

"Cassandra, it is time. You may come in or open the door."

Confused Cassandra stood in front of the light trying to figure out what it meant. She knew there were no doors for she had watched them all disappear. Was this just another trick her mind was playing on her? She then sensed something to her right. When she turned her head there stood one lonely door. She stepped a little closer and noticed this one looked newer than the others. Not understanding, she turned back towards the light and asked, "If I choose the door what will I find?"

"I cannot answer that of which you already know."

"Home...," Cassandra let out with a hint of joy. "It leads home."

"You have made your choice."

"What?" Cassandra barely spoke. Before she had a chance to ask any more questions the light was sucked back into the darkness, leaving her alone. Now she was left wondering how she could have made a choice when she didn't even give an answer. Hoping the choice that was left truly led to home she turned back towards her only way out of the darkness.

She stood in front of the door staring at it when she saw little streams of light pushing their way through the frame. Slowly she walked closer as the silence grew almost deafening. As she approached a faint erythematic beeping could be heard. She listened intensely and realized it did not match any of the alarms or timers in her house. What could be making that sound and where was it coming from? She crept closer to get the answers.

All of a sudden, a displeasing smell engulfed her nose. It was a mixture of disinfectant, plastic tubing and one more thing she could not describe, but taste. When she got close enough to reach the knob she paused for a moment. Did she really want to know what was behind the door with that nasty smell? She glanced around hoping there was another way out. When she saw none, she turned back and let out a small quiet sigh. Cautiously she raised her hand and as she grabbed the knob, she felt a stabbing pain in the back of her hand. Before she had time to react, she saw a plastic tube appear and grow longer from where the pain originated. Frantically she tried to yank it out, but then she started to gasp.

With both hands Cassandra grabbed her throat. As she struggled for each breath her body finally collapsed. Not understanding what was going on she tried to get back up, but her body wouldn't move. It seemed the only part of her that still worked was her eyes, but even those had their limits. Able to see what was happening to her she watched as a larger tube appeared and hovered over her face. She tried to close her eyes as it drew in closer, but unfortunately, they functioned as if they were glued in place.

As she watched the tube descend, she could feel a hand press on the sides of her mouth and knew it wasn't her own. Unable to stop what was happening, her mouth opened and the pressure on her tongue allowed the large thick tube to slide down her airway. She felt it scratch the sides of her throat as it slid down then stopped briefly. After it was re-angled it continued to be pushed downward. Once it finally stopped, she heard the sounds of air pumping and soon she was able to breathe again. Relief swept over her followed by a nasty taste of plastic and garlic, and before she knew it her eyes finally closed.

After awhile Cassandra felt her body being lifted then placed upon something soft. The only explanation she could think of for the comfort she felt was she was home. She tried to open her eyes, but they would not budge. Then she tried to open her mouth to speak.

However, the obstruction in her airway still remained. All she had left were her ears. She listened carefully to her surroundings and from the sounds of compressed air, bleeping, and the intercom she figured she must be in a hospital. But what happened that led her here? She allowed the sounds to fade into the background as she drifted back into the darkness.

The Beginning

The smell of freshly brewed coffee filled the apartment as the late autumn sun rose. As the aroma drifted down the hall and into the bathroom Cassandra turned off the shower. She then reached for the small towel she had hanging over the shower door and wrapped it around her head. After tucking the ends in tightly so it would not fall, she opened the shower door and cautiously stepped out onto the bathroom rug. She stood in one place while she grabbed another towel from the towel rack to dry off with.

Once her whole body was dried, she wrapped the towel around her body then took a step over to the sink. As she looked up at the mirror, she noticed she was unable to see herself because it was covered with steam. In order to clear out the bathroom she stepped back into the shower and opened the small window. The cool breeze from outside forced its way in, taking over the space occupied by the heat. As she began to shiver, she clinched tighter to the towel around her. She then stepped back out of the shower and wiped her wet feet off on the rug before leaving the bathroom to get dressed.

Since her apartment was small, she only had a few steps from the bathroom to her bedroom. When she entered, she looked down at the clothes she had laid across her bed earlier. Satisfied with her choice she made her way over to her double dresser. She opened the right top drawer and pulled out the first pair of underwear which lay on top along with one of her bras. Holding the items in one hand she closed the door with the other. As she stood between the dresser and the bed, she tossed the bra onto her outer clothes leaving her with only her underwear. Even though she was alone she still had a sense of modesty about her, so she slipped her feet into her underwear and carefully pulled them up her legs with her towel still on.

After readjusting her towel, she sat down at the edge of her bed to finish getting dressed. As usual the first thing she picked up was her socks. It was important to make sure her feet were warm before she continued. Next, she grabbed her bra. She tugged on her towel then allowed it to drop to her waist so she could put it on. She wrapped the band underneath her breast making sure the clasps were in front. Once they were hooked together, she spun the bra around until she had the cups in front and put her arms into the straps.

Now that her undergarments were in place she grabbed her jeans and slid her legs into them. She pulled the jeans up her legs until she was able to see her socks. It was now time for her to stand up and pull them on the rest of the way. After zipping up her jeans all that was left was her sweatshirt. She turned back to the bed and leaned over to pick up her white hooded sweatshirt. After sliding her arms through the sleeves and pulling the large hole over her head she stood in front of her full-length mirror hanging on her bedroom door.

She stood wearing the typical attire expected of a college student, but today she wouldn't be attending her classes. No, today she had a very important appointment. So, after picking up the towel from the bed and readjusting the one on her head, she went back into the bathroom to finish getting ready.

By the time she entered the bathroom the steam had gone. Able to see herself in the mirror she automatically reached for the bottle of foundation on the countertop. She shook the bottle three times then when it came time to open the cap she paused. Should she even bother putting on her makeup? She pondered on the question for a moment then remembered the uncertainty of the day's events to come and replaced the bottle on the counter.

With one less thing to do Cassandra lowered her head letting the towel drop into her hands. She took hold of it then placed it on the back of her head and began to rub the towel through her hair. When she was done, she flipped her head back up and placed the towel on the rack next to the other to dry. As she looked into the mirror at her mangled hair, she pulled out one of the top drawers and reached in for her hairbrush.

Stroke after stroke she brushed her hair until it was straight. She then traded the brush for a comb. As she ran the comb through her hair, she decided today would be a good day to put it back into a ponytail. It was easy, quick and allowed her hair a break from the damaging extreme heat of the hair dryer. She continued to comb her hair back into the hand waiting to grab it. When she had all of her hair tightly held, she laid the comb down on the counter then grabbed three rubber bands to hold it in place.

After putting everything away she took one last real look at herself in the mirror. There was something missing. The normal happy glow she had about her had been replaced with uncertainty. She looked into her own eyes and hoped by morning's end it would return.

From there she headed into the kitchen and in between the refrigerator and sink she opened the small narrow cabinet to claimed one of her two favorite white coffee cups her mother had given her. She checked it out to make sure it was clean then took it over to the coffee pot. After setting it down upon the counter and before pouring the brown liquid into it, she grabbed for the sugar container.

Cassandra could never drink her coffee black, so she scooped in three spoonfuls of sugar followed by three heaping spoonfuls of the dry non-dairy creamer. Now she was ready to add the coffee to the mixture. As she looked down into her cup while stirring, she smiled. For some reason that moment reminded her of the time she had to use her coffee as her science project.

It was her freshman year in college and for chemistry class she was supposed to bring in a liquid to evaluate its PH balance. She walked into her class tired from being up all-night studying and doing homework for her other classes. It wasn't until she had reached her stool and sat down did, she remember her lab project. As her classmates filtered in, she began to worry about getting a failing grade. Everyone had brought something to be assessed except her. Disappointed in herself she reached for her traveler's mug full of coffee. It was then she got the idea to use it.

After a small lecture from her instructor, it was time to move onto the project. Everyone grabbed their liquids and placed them in a straight line on the counter in the back of the room. In groups of three they went from one liquid to the other and discussed the results. So far, the results have come back either acidic or alkaline. Finally, it was time to evaluate her project. Nervous, she dipped the PH strip into her coffee as her classmates guessed it would come out acidic. But when she pulled the strip out the results both stunned and amazed her classmates. It read a perfectly balanced PH7. Everyone then asked her how she did it and the only answer she could come up with was she liked her life balanced.

Balanced was not how she would describe her life now. Still holding onto her cup with both hands she walked over to the calendar hanging from a push pin placed in the wall of her kitchen/dining room. She stared at the red circle on today's date and raised the cup to her lips. As she took a sip she thought 'If only I hadn't fought so hard to go to college far from home.' She then lowered her cup and sighed.

With the image of her mother still in her head she walked over to the table built large enough for two and sat down. After placing her cup upon the table, she reached over to the windowsill and unplugged her cell phone from its charger. She flipped her phone open and stared down at the picture she had chosen for her screen. There staring back at her with dancing green eyes and a proud smile was her mother. She smiled back as she pondered on whether or not she should call her. After a moment of thought she knew she wasn't ready to tell her mother what was going on until she knew herself.

As she closed her phone she glanced down at the time then up at the calendar. She raised her cup up to her lips and sipped as her mind began to shift back to the day when she first found out something was wrong.

It had been three years to the day since she had gone in for her yearly pap, but what transpired that day changed her life forever. She sat on the examination table waiting for her doctor to return. Something was found but she didn't know what. Her doctor told her she would have it tested and come right back with the results. Thinking it couldn't be anything too bad she grabbed a couple of magazines and thumbed through them. She was in the middle of reading an article on how to keep a relationship moving forward when her doctor walked into the room. At first, she was happy to see her because she wanted to get the green light to get dressed and go home, but without emotion her doctor blurted out she had the Human Papilloma virus. Fighting back tears of disbelief she asked her doctor what the next step was. Her doctor replied by advising her that she needed further testing to see how severe it was.

Since that day she had endured many uncomfortable scrapings of her cervix. And after every visit she had been told to come back in six months to see if it had healed itself. Unfortunately, it had not, and after three years her doctor suggested further testing which she complied with two weeks ago. Today would be the day she would find out from her doctor if her HPV had turned cancerous.

Bracing herself for the longest day of her life, Cassandra got up and made herself another cup of coffee. As she drank her second cup the seconds finally turned into minutes. She picked up her cell phone from the table and checked the time. She read 9:30 am and she knew her appointment was at 10.

It was time for her to warm up her old beat-up Honda, which by the grace of God still served its purpose. She put on her coat and picked up the keys from the end table closest to the door. As she stepped outside the wind howled as it whipped through the trees. She covered her face with the hood of her coat as she made her way to the open parking lot. When she reached her car, she unlocked her door then sat inside and turned it on.

It would be at least another ten minutes before her windows would defrost entirely, so to occupy her time she turned on the radio. The heavy alternative rock that blared through her speakers did nothing to help her mood. Needing to relax, she quickly turned the dial until she found something more classical. As she waited, she allowed the mellow sound coming from her radio seep into her body and she closed her eyes.

When she opened them again, she noticed her windows had finally defogged enough to see out of, so she buckled herself in and slowly backed out of her parking space. After clearing all the other cars around her she straightened out her steering wheel and drove to the end of the parking lot. From there she turned left and drove down the small narrow back street trying hard not to hit any of the parked cars parked along the side of it. As she got closer to the main street, she lightly touched her brakes and rolled up to the stop. Looking left she waited for the line of cars to pass then when all was clear she turned right.

As she drove down Main Street she glanced briefly to her left at her school. Her thoughts were upon what she was missing and if she could make it up when a gust of wind picked carried a leaf into her windshield. "There goes another suicide leaf," she said out loud.

It was little things and comments like that one that reminded her of her mother. She smiled as she remembered her mother always had something to say regarding the weather. A few of her favorites were angels having pillow fights for snow and God flashing his flashlight then stubbing his toe in the darkness making him rumble for thunder and lightening. Even though she was older and understood what caused snow and how thunderstorms were formed, somehow just thinking like her mother made her smile just a little.

Before long, the mile drive to the clinic was at its end and she pulled into the left turn lane. By now most of the cars on the road were at their destinations so she was able to turn without waiting and pulled into the parking lot. The one nice thing about having a morning appointment was she could park in front. After rolling into the spot closest to the door, she put her car into park then turned off the engine. Next, she searched her large bag, that she called a purse, for her cell phone. Funny how things you place on top always seem to move themselves to the bottom. Once she had her phone in hand she glanced at it one more time. She made it with five minutes to spare.

Nervous, she fumbled with the door handle then once the door opened, she got out. The wind whipped through her still wet ponytail smacking it on her cheek. Hopefully for her this would be the worst part of her day. After locking her car door, she walked up to the door and drew in a deep breath before entering.

A bell rang as she swung opened the door prompting a warm greeting from the lady behind the counter. To be polite she returned the greeting with a slight smile as she walked towards her to check in. She had seen this lady many times but never could remember her name, but that was okay for it seemed the lady didn't remember hers either. The lady asked for her name then handed her the form she needed to sign on a clipboard. After signing the form and handing it back she took one of the seats across from the fish tank that was mounted into the wall. She had always thought it to be an odd place to put such a thing, but she did find some peace watching the fish swim around in the live piece of art. Unfortunately, before she had time to relax the assistant opened the door and called out her name.

Cassandra followed the woman through the door and down the hall to a small room where she took her usual place upon the makeshift bed. As the woman wrapped the black band around her arm to check her vital signs she wondered if she already knew her fate. She watched the woman's facial expressions hoping to catch some kind of hint. But the woman showed no signs of knowing anything except her job as she placed the thermometer in her mouth.

Before long, the thermometer was pulled out and the black band unwrapped from her arm. Everything seemed to be normal. She watched as the assistant put everything back in its place then opened one of the cabinet doors next to the sink and pulled out a gown. Knowing what was next she reached out and took the gown and placed it on her lap. She waited until the assistant left then quickly undressed down to the bare minimum. After unfolding the gown, she stuck her hands through the sleeves and wrapped it around her. When she had the strings tied, she sat back on the bed to wait. Her wait didn't take long for a faint knock came to the door. "Come in."

"How are you today, Cassandra?" asked the doctor.

"I'm fine."

"As you know I received your test results back from your last visit. But before I go over it with you, I would like to perform one more routine check."

"Ok." Cassandra lay down and placed her feet into the stirrups like usual. Yet, what her doctor considered routine was not to her. She knew today was different. She knew today she would find out whether or not she would need surgery.

When Cassandra stepped out of the clinic the once promising day resembled night. Dark ominous clouds had taken over the sky and the wind howled furiously. As she stepped off the sidewalk into the parking lot the wind pushed her against her car. She managed to hold onto her purse and gathered her keys. After she unlocked the door, she pulled up on the latch. She tried hard to open the door and when she finally did the wind forced it closed.

"Damn! I don't need this right now," she cried out as she looked up into the sky. After lowering her head and taking a deep breath she tried again. This time she quickly wedged her purse between the door and the door frame of her car. With a large enough opening she squeezed her way into her car. She managed to only endure a few scrapes and bruises on her way in. The only problem now was getting her legs inside, so she desperately tried to hold the door at bay while she pulled them in.

With the outside world finally closed off she tossed her purse into the passenger's seat then sat with the keys in her hand staring at the steering wheel. Everything around soon turned into a blur as her mind drifted back to the outcome of her visit. How could life play such a cruel joke on her? She had always told everyone she never wanted children, but now that she couldn't it tore her apart.

Tears began to spill down upon Cassandra's cheeks as she turned on her car. The classical music that helped soothe her mood earlier only made things worse, so she reached out to turn it off. As her fingertips touched the knob it fell off then slipped through her fingers finally resting upon the floor. Then as if things couldn't get any worse the rain began to pour. She let out a deep sigh as she stretched over to the passenger's side of the car. Fumbling around with her hand she searched for the missing knob on the floorboard. When she found it, she picked it up then wiped away the water from her face. She then replaced the knob back and successfully turned off the radio.

After turning on her wipers she leaned closer to the windshield and looked up. The storm outside seemed to reflect her mood. Her thoughts then turned back towards her mother once more. "The angels are crying with me."

Her mother was her lifeline and if she was going to survive this day she had to call. She grabbed her purse off the passenger's seat then rummaged through it for her cell phone. After finding it she tossed her purse back over to the passenger's seat and flipped it open. As quickly as her fingers could move, she dialed her mother's number then held it up to her ear. As the phone rang, she backed out of the parking space and headed towards the entrance.

After looking towards her left for traffic she pulled out of the parking lot. She had only gone a block when she heard her mother answer. "Mom..."

"What's wrong baby girl?"

"How do you..."

"I can hear it in your voice. I love you too."

"I miss you so much right now," Cassandra stated as she tried to hold back her tears.

"I miss you too baby girl."

Cassandra tried to concentrate on her driving as she thought about how to tell her mother her news. She was never good about coming straight out with things, so instead she asked, "Will you be mad at me if I can't give you grandchildren?"

As the stream of tears ran from her eyes the rain drove harder towards her windshield.

"No, baby girl, I love you for who you are not what you can give."

"Mom..." sniffle, "I have cancer."

"Do you want me to come down?"

"Yes, could you?" Cassandra did not hear her mother's answer for a flash of light bolted in front of her. When she was finally able to see again, she quickly slammed on her brakes as a tree fell onto the road in front of her.

"Cassandra, are you there? Cassandra...Cassandra..."

Surrounded by darkness Cassandra could hear the faint sounds of saws while every now and then light penetrated the blackness behind her eyelids. She tried to open her eyes but was overcome by an excruciating pain in her chest. After deciding to keep her eyes closed, she began to feel faint as her breath became shallow. She now faces the decision whether to endure the pain or allow herself to succumb to the darkness.

Everything Falls

It had been the longest six hours the Blanchard's had ever traveled to see Cassandra. And now they were finally pulling into the parking lot of the hospital. As Steve drove around to find a parking spot close to the entrance his mother began to sweep again. It tore at his heart to see her in such pain and there was nothing he could do to ease it. Cassandra was her baby, her pride and joy, and hearing the accident when it happened made it even worse. All he knew was what his mother had managed to ramble between sobs. So, expecting the worst he rolled into the first spot available.

By the time the car had come to rest Mrs. Blanchard was already unbuckled and had her door opened. With tissue in hand, she swiped her purse from the floorboard and exited the car. She rushed across the parking lot towards the emergency entrance leaving her other children behind. Nothing else mattered but to see her baby girl.

The large glass doors automatically opened as she stepped in front of them. And once inside she began her quest. She quickly spotted the visitor's counter and approached the middle-aged woman behind it. "I am looking for my daughter. She was brought here by ambulance a few hours ago."

"What is her name?"

"Cassandra Blanchard, the EMT told me this was where they were taking her."

"Yes, there she is. Go straight down this hall," the lady pointed to her left, "and follow the signs to surgery."

"Thank you." As Mrs. Blanchard turned to go her adult children burst through the entrance. Knowing they would follow, she walked away from the counter and headed down the hall. As she sprinted towards the designated waiting area she feared the worst. Her daughter should have been out of surgery by now. But then she remembered small hospitals sometimes use the same waiting area for those in recovery and out-patient. With a little hope to cling onto she pressed onward.

It wasn't much further down the hall when they came upon the surgery. And while her children walked into the waiting room Mrs. Blanchard walked up to the nurse's station. She didn't have to wait long before one of them acknowledged her presence and asked if she could help. After setting her purse on the counter she swiped a tissue from the opened box, placed conveniently for those who needed them, then gave out her daughter's information once again. As the nurse informed her that her daughter was still in surgery, she wiped away the tears threatening to run down her cheeks. And even though it wasn't the news she had hoped for she thanked the nurse before headed into the waiting room.

Upon rejoining her other children, she was thankful there was no one else in the room when she broke the news. As she sat down, she could tell they were tired, but no one wanted to sleep for fear of missing the doctor when he came out of surgery. She tilted her head upwards to look as if she was staring at the scenic picture on the wall. But in reality, she was playing back the last conversation she had with Cassandra. She could tell Cassandra was deeply upset and in no condition to drive. So why did Cassandra call her while driving? And why did she not tell her to hang up and call her back when she got home? If only she had not kept her on the phone. Maybe, just maybe none of this would have happened.

Still, she had heard Cassandra's scream followed by the smashing of glass and metal. Chills ran up her spine as she remembered how she continued to call out Cassandra's name, but everything had gone quiet. Instead of hanging up she stayed on the phone and after a few minutes she finally heard more sounds. She continued to listen to the entire rescue and when it was quiet again, she thought she heard one of the emergency responders pick up the phone. Hoping they could hear her she called out, and by the grace of God someone had. She told the

EMT on the other end who she was and in return he gave her the name of the hospital where they were transporting her to. As guilt set in, her son scooted closer and wrapped his arm around her shoulders.

"Mom it's no one's fault," Steven stated. He pulled his mother closer to him and allowed her to place her head on his shoulder to cry.

While her brother stroked their mother's hair for comfort Vicky walked across the room to grab a box of tissues from one of the tables. When she rejoined her family, she knelt down in front of her mother and handed her a few tissues she had just pulled out of the box. As her mother grabbed the tissues out of her hand the doctor entered the waiting room, catching her attention.

"Are you the Blanchard family?"

Mrs. Blanchard raised her head and wiped her nose before answering, "I'm Cassandra's mother."

"Mrs. Blanchard, I am Dr. Rutledge." As he introduced himself, he walked closer to the family. "Do you want to go somewhere where we can speak in private?"

Since there was no one else in the room Mrs. Blanchard kindly refused the offer. "How is my daughter?"

"Your daughter has been in surgery for more than six hours," Dr. Rutledge started then paused. He knew the next words out of his mouth would be hard on the family so he wanted to make sure he explained it in a way they would understand. "We managed to repair both of her legs, but I'm afraid the injuries to her spinal cord will render them useless."

A little relieved Mrs. Blanchard grabbed a few more tissues from the box her daughter still held in her hand and dried her eyes. "So, what you are saying is she is paralyzed."

"Not exactly."

Watching the roller coaster of emotions in her mother's eyes Vicky quickly stood up in frustration and anger as she asked, "Is she or is she not?"

Steven grabbed hold of his sister's arm hoping to calm her down for their mother's sake. Then in a calm whisper he begged her to hear the doctor out.

Understanding what they were going through Dr. Rutledge continued, "Yes she is paralyzed. However, she had suffered severe head trauma."

"What are you saying?" Steven interrupted as he grabbed hold of his mother's hand.

"It is my deepest regret to inform you Cassandra has fallen into a deep coma and might not recover."

In that instant the three clung to each other. The tissue box passed around. Was there no hope insight? How were they going to celebrate Cassandra's favorite holiday without her? Mrs. Blanchard refused to except the thought of her daughter never returning home and looked up to find the doctor still standing in the room. "Can we go see her?"

"She will be in recovery for about another hour, but I will allow one person to visit."

Without argument Mrs. Blanchard stood up and took hold of the doctor's arm for strength. When she was ready, he led her through the double doors and down the corridor. For her it was the loneliest walk of her life. Stifling back tears, she tried to prepare herself for what she was about to see. But the only images her mind allowed in were the cute little girl who had danced her way into everyone's hearts.

One of those images took her back to the day when Cassandra first decided to try out for the dance team her freshman year in high school. Cassandra had come home after the first day of tryouts, worried she might not make the team because she was not as slim as the rest of the girls. It broke her heart to hear her daughter so insecure about herself. So, she sat her down next to her on the couch and reassured her that if she gave one hundred percent or more of herself there would be no doubt she would make the team. The very next day she drove to the school to bring her daughter a jug of water and as all the girls were warming up in the gym she decided to pull the coach aside. She never mentioned her name or her daughter's, but the coach knew immediately who she was talking about. Much to her relief the coach eased her concern by telling her she based her decisions on talent and determination. The coach also added she would not be surprised if Cassandra ended up as captain her senior year. With that little hope she returned home and kept the conversation a secret. By the end of the week Cassandra came home with a glee of excitement and she knew her daughter had done what she had set out to do. She held onto that smile as they turned the corner towards the recovery room.

When they reached the second door Dr. Rutledge stopped and stated, "You may go in, but remember she is in a coma and will not be able to respond to you."

"Thank you so much," whispered Mrs. Blanchard as she stared at the door while it was opened for her. Everything and everybody disappeared the moment she stepped into the room. Cautiously she walked closer to the curtain not sure of what she would see. Afraid of how she would react, she slowly pulled back the curtain. The woman lying there was indeed her daughter, but her long golden locks were replaced by bandages, and her beautiful face bore scrapes and bruises. Saddened by what she saw she quietly walked closer to the bed.

Upon seeing a chair in the corner, she pulled it in closer next to her daughter and sat down. The guilt of it not being her began to overwhelm her as she grabbed hold of her daughter's hand. She then placed her head upon her daughter's lap and allowed herself to pray. "Dear God please give back to me my little girl. She has so much to give."

For a second Mrs. Blanchard thought she felt her daughter's hand grip hers. When she opened her eyes and looked down towards her hand, she realized it was only her imagination. Disappointed, she lifted her head off of her daughter's lap and with her other hand she lightly brushed her cheek. She gazed at her daughter wishing she could take her place. Overwhelmed by tears she reluctantly let go of her daughter's hand to wipe them away. She then leaned back into the chair and closed her eyes to pray some more.

In the midst of one of her prayers Mrs. Blanchard felt an arm on her shoulder. She reopened her eyes and looked up to find Dr. Rutledge standing next to her. As she stared up at him through puffy eyes, he sadly informed her she had to return to the waiting room while he checked on his patient. Though her heart was saddened she accepted his kind offer to help her up. With her arm wrapped around the sleeve of his long white coat he escorted her to the door where a pleasant nurse awaited to guide her back to her family.

In the waiting room Steve had allowed Vicky to rest upon his shoulder. While she napped, he kept a visual on the doorway. He had been the rock of the family since their father's passing and today would be no exception. At least that was what he had hoped until he saw his mother enter the room. With a quick shrug of his shoulder, he nudged Vicky awake. As she stirred, he got up and walked over to aid his mother. He placed a comforting arm around her shoulders then gently guided her to the chair next to Vicky.

From there Vicky took her mother's arm and helped her sit down. "How does she look?"

That was a question Mrs. Blanchard wanted to avoid. She wanted her children to remember their sister the way she was, not what she saw. So instead of describing her condition she just answered, "Peaceful."

Steve quickly understood his mother's code and picked up the empty chair next to his mother and replanted it in front of her. Without saying a word, he sat down and stretched out his arms. As he lowered his head and closed his eyes, he felt his mother and sister take hold of his hands. Together they prayed for their loved one's recovery.

After a complete check-up on his patient Dr. Rutledge entered the waiting room. There he found the Blanchard family huddled close together in silence. He had seen this reaction many times before, and it always touched his heart. But it also made the news he was about to give harder. Respecting their privacy, he stayed back and waited. It wasn't until the son raised his head and acknowledged his presence that he approached. "I'm sorry, but the prognosis is not good. We have moved Cassandra into another room so all of you can visit her."

After handing his mother another tissue Steve held tightly to her hand, bracing her for the answer to the question he was about to ask, "How long?"

"I'm afraid she won't make it through the night." As expected, the wailing began, and Dr. Rutledge pulled out the notebook from his pocket. He wrote down the room number then tore it out and handed it to the son. Since there was nothing more he could say or do to help this family he respectfully walked away.

Clutching the piece of paper in his hand Steve wrapped his arms around both his mother and sister. He knew he had to become the rock once again. And with his baby sister slipping away there wasn't much time. "We should go see her now."

Agreeing with her son, Mrs. Blanchard pushed her sadness deep within herself. There would be enough time for tears later, but for now she needed to be there for her baby girl. She wiped her eyes and nose then wrapped her arm around her son's. On their way out of the waiting room she leaned over slightly and snagged another box of tissue from one of the tables.

Steve held his mother close to him while Vicky followed closely behind. As they walked down the hall he took a quick glance at the piece of paper, Room 225. Knowing they had to reach the second floor he searched for the nearest elevator.

Just a little farther down the hall he spotted an elevator sign with an arrow pointing left. As they turned the corner his mother's sniffles had all but subsided. Eager to get her to her baby girl he urgently pressed the up button. And to his surprise it immediately dinged. Shortly there after the tall metallic double doors parted and he ushered his mother inside with Vicky in swift pursuit. As the doors began to close, he took another look at the piece of paper to make sure he pressed the correct floor, number 2.

The elevator ride was a quiet one. No one wanted to say anything for fear of upsetting the others. When the elevator finally stopped, and the doors opened, the three stepped out and stood looking forward at the sign on the wall. They turned to their right and headed to the end of the hall where they found another sign directing them to go left. As they walked down the hall everyone's eyes were focused to their right for that was where the odd numbered rooms were located. Upon the third door they read 225. Before entering they took hold of each other's hands and said one last prayer. When the prayer came to an end Steve opened the door and allowed his mother to enter first.

As Mrs. Blanchard entered, she noticed nothing had changed. All the machines and tubing were still intact, but this time it was different. She knew her daughter was slipping away and there was nothing she could do to stop it. When she reached the bed, she stood over her daughter and took her hand. She then leaned over and whispered, "Cassandra."

Steve had just placed a chair for Vicky on the other side of Cassandra's bed when he heard his mother's shaky voice. Alarmed, he looked up and upon seeing her body tremble he rushed around the bed. Just as he got behind her, she turned and fell into his chest weeping.

Vicky acted quickly and pulled up another chair for their mother. She stayed to help Steve gently lower her down into it. When their mother was settled, she gently placed her hand on his arm and said, "You go ahead. I'll stay with mom."

After placing a kiss on the top of his mother's head he turned to face the little sister who had always supported him while growing up. As he looked down at her he took her hand in his. "Hey, it's Steve, and yes we are all here to visit you." He paused for a moment and glanced back at his mother to make sure she was all right. When she nodded, he turned back and continued, "Do you remember back in high school when I played football? I never told you how much it meant to me that you not only performed during half-time but stayed to cheer me on when all of your friends left to get ready for the dance. I can still see your smiling face up in the bleachers with my number painted on your cheek. You were so proud of me, and I was proud of you. Please don't forget me."

Vicky watched her brother pat Cassandra's hand then walked away to the other side of the room. It was her turn, but she didn't know what to say. She was the oldest of the three and had already graduated from high school by the time her sister had started. Also, she had been resentful and jealous of the way her mother favored Cassandra. With that in mind she knew of only one way to redeem herself, so she leaned over her sister, placed a kiss upon her cheek and whispered, "Please forgive me."

Waiting patiently for her oldest to finish, Mrs. Blanchard sat listening to the storm raging outside. It was as if God had already made his decision and shared her pain. She knew now she had to give up her beautiful little girl, so when her other daughter had joined her son, she graciously stood up and walked over to her youngest. For her final farewell she leaned close to her daughter's face then whispered in her ear, "May these angels' wings take you to a better life." Then upon her cheek she placed her final act of love in the form of a Butterfly Kiss.

A New Beginning

Feeling angel's wings brush against her face Cassandra found herself standing in the void once more. Again, she saw a bright light, only this time it approached her. Now understanding and unafraid she stepped in.

The dishwasher hummed its own musical tune as Cassandra leaned against the counter drying her hands. With a quiet sigh she thought about all the other things left to do before Christmas morning. There were presents to wrap, stockings to fill, and cookies to decorate. As her eyes fixated on the cooling cookies a pair of brown shoes entered the kitchen. They crept closer towards Cassandra as if on a mission. Then just inches away they stopped.

Cassandra seemed oblivious to the intruder. At least until she heard a creek in close proximity. She nearly jumped out of her skin, but when her eyes fell upon her husband, she snapped him with the towel. "Damn you, Sean! You practically scared the living daylights out of me."

"Whoa, wait a minute;" Sean cried out when he saw his wife reading the towel for another strike, "It's not my fault you didn't see me come in."

It was true. He had been in plain sight. So why did she not see or hear him? While she pondered on the question her husband went back to the cupboard. But it didn't take long for her to realize she had been distracted. She placed the towel on the counter then with sincerity she apologized. His warm gentle smile told her he had accepted. And when he went back to collect the last two mugs she was reminded of the night's ritual.

With her husband taking care of the hot cocoa, she decided to take a break. As she walked towards the dining room she felt a slight prick on her buttock. In a flash she spun around. And when she saw the devious grin on her husband's face, she couldn't believe he had just pinched her. Realizing his playful intensions, she shook her finger at him then turned and walked away.

She entered the dining room as the sound of running water reached her ears. It seemed everything was running smoothly. That was until she noticed the tablecloth was slightly draped more over to one side. For her everything had a place, and everything had to be in place. So unable to control the urge she walked over and fixed it. With that now out of the way she headed for her resting place.

As she made her way into the living room, she was surprised to find her eight-year-old son and six-year-old daughter quietly putting a puzzle together on the floor. Their polite behavior made her wonder if they were behaving because they were told to. Or was it due to Santa's impending visit? Either way she was pleased to have the quietness. With the desire to keep it that way she carefully walked past them.

When she finally reached the sofa, she plopped down. Then after taking a moment to breathe, she leaned towards the coffee table and picked up the book she had placed there earlier. Ready to pick up where she left off, she scooted back and raised her knees close to her. She then rested the book against her legs and was about to open to the marked page when something caught the corner of her eye.

Through the small opening between the curtains, she saw a bright icy white film around the windowsill. Sure, delight bubbled within her as she turned towards her children and said, "It looks like snow this year kids."

###

Thank you for reading my book. If you enjoyed it, please take the time to leave me a review at your favorite retailer.

Thank you,

Linda Brown

About the Author

Linda L Brown was born and raised in the wonderful state of Oregon. Its distinct four seasons provide the settings for many of her books. She has had a passion for writing since junior high, in which she drafted short stories. A few years after High school she got together with Debi Lundin and wrote a romance novel, "Phantom's Flame", which was published in 2007. Since then, she has ventured out to author novels on her own.

Linda has one other eBook available online "Ashley and The Griffin".

She enjoys reading Romance novels from pirate to steam punk and mysteries. Favorite reads include Agatha Christie (Miss Marple and Poirot), Sir Arthur Conan Doyle (Sherlock Holmes), and Kate Cross (The Clockwork Agents).

www.ingramcontent.com/pod-product-compliance
Lightning Source LLC
Chambersburg PA
CBHW051208160726
47994CB00002B/509